Jealousy & Yams
Stories From Hartford

Amanda Hamm

Jealousy & Yams is a work of fiction. All names, characters, places, events, etc are products
of the author's imagination or are used fictitiously.

ISBN: 978-0-98506596-6

Chapter 1

The monstrosity pulling into Gloria Foster's driveway was clearly not her son's idea. She went outside to get a better look at the bright red pickup truck as Luke climbed out of the driver's seat. "Hi, Mom," he said.

"Luke, what happened?" She narrowed her eyes at the vehicle as though daring it to explain itself.

"Dad's old Camry needed more work than they first thought. I told you I might be getting a new car."

"You said might... and this is not a car."

"I saw Uncle Rob yesterday."

Gloria shook her head. "We're still talking about the truck. Who talked you into it?"

"I like it." Luke pushed the button on his keychain and the lock clicked loudly before he started spinning the ring around his index finger.

"It's completely different from what you've been driving the last ten years."

Luke nodded at the truck. "I think that's why it caught my eye."

His mom sighed. She supposed he would simply have to live with this truck that someone had unloaded on him. "What did Rob want?"

"He just stopped by the office to say hello. I guess he was visiting someone in Hartford."

"Well, let's go inside to talk. You know I can't stand around in the sun." Gloria Foster held her hand up between her face and the sun as she said this. The woman was fifty-two, but could easily pass for forty. She had been following an elaborate skin care routine since her twenties and recently took the next step, chemical peels. She changed her hair color every few years and was currently sporting a platinum blond style, held in place just above her shoulders with copious amounts of hair spray. She was a fan of business suits and wore a royal blue one with a knee-length

1

skirt and fitted jacket even though it was Saturday and she had no plans to leave the house.

Luke was exactly half his mother's age and spent far less than half as much time on his appearance. The sun put gold flecks in his light brown hair. It was thick and wavy and presently very short. His mom had suggested only the previous week that it was time for a haircut. He gave his key ring a final spin and pushed up the bottom of his plain gray T-shirt enough to stuff his keys into his jeans pocket. He followed his mom into her house.

Lunch was already on the dining room table. Chicken salad in a crystal bowl sat waiting to be applied to the sliced bread on a silver platter. There were a few lemon slices in the glass pitcher of ice water and the table was set perfectly for two with cloth napkins that matched the blue and white checked place mats. The meal itself was modest, but Gloria Foster believed in the power of presentation.

"This looks great," Luke said as he took his seat.

They bowed their heads briefly in silent prayer and then Luke picked up the spoon to make his sandwich.

"We shipped an update to Triangle Ships yesterday."

Gloria made herself a very dainty sandwich. "That's good," she said. "I believe you said Friday was the goal."

Luke nodded. "Right on time. We added a new destination planet and mostly defensive upgrades." He knew his mother's support of his company didn't yet extend to playing the games they made so she didn't fully understand the details. He also knew she'd still want to hear the details so that she could later prove she had been paying attention.

"Do you think people will buy those upgrades?" she asked.

"I hope so. That's why we offer them."

Gloria smiled at her son. He had only started the company a year ago and she hoped it wouldn't be much longer before they put out a game that interested her. He did seem to enjoy his work though. His pleasant mood made her decide that it was a good time to bring up the subject she wanted to discuss. "I talked to Elaine Johnson this week."

Luke nodded. "Did you see the thing in the paper yesterday about the new bank branch right down the street from you?"

Gloria closed her eyes for a moment. "I did. But I was going to tell you what Elaine Johnson told me."

"Oh, sorry."

"It's fine." Luke's mom waved off his apology. "She and I talked for quite a while actually, and during the course of it, I found out about a girl who might be good for you."

"Really?" Luke's voice was flat and his eyes didn't leave his plate.

Gloria pressed on anyway. "I guess she works at a nursing home or something. She goes to our church and it sounds as though she inherited a decent amount of money from an aunt last year."

"I see." Luke stuffed the rest of his sandwich into his mouth to avoid saying anything else right away. His mom was always warning him that women might pretend to like him for his money. He thought her fears were ridiculously unfounded. He had been on three dates since college and none had led to second dates. There were times when he almost wished someone would pretend to like him. It would not be for the millions of dollars at his disposal if no woman would stick around long enough to find out about it.

"So what do you think?" Gloria prompted her son.

"What do I think of this girl I know nothing about?"

"You know that at least with her you wouldn't have to worry about... she wouldn't be in need of..."

"Mom, you know as well as I do that people who have money can still want more. Besides, it's not as though I go around advertising our wealth. I hope to have a reasonable opinion of a girl's character before I say something."

"You don't have to advertise things when you insist on living in that itty bitty town. You don't think everyone in Hartford started talking about you like some sort of Mr. Bingley the same day you bought the house?"

Luke tipped his head to the side. "Is that a Jane Austen reference?"

"My point is that you can't hide it and that it doesn't matter anyway because when I talked to Elaine I arranged for her to introduce me to Rebecca so that I could introduce her to you."

"Rebecca, huh?" It was obvious that this introduction would make his mom happy and Luke didn't see the harm in playing along. She wasn't asking anything as bad as a blind date. He could say hello to a young woman at church. This Rebecca would lose interest as soon as he said something ridiculous anyway.

"Yes, Rebecca Hilson. I hear she's *very* pretty." Gloria Foster nodded as though this was a good thing. Luke wasn't too concerned with her appearance, but the name meant something to him.

3

"I think that's what Zander called the haunted house."

"He called it what?" Gloria asked. She had gotten the acceptance she wanted and could switch gears.

"Zander is the kid who mows my lawn."

"I know."

"He was telling me about a house in town that everyone says is haunted. I think he called it the old Hilson house."

"Could be a relative. It's something you can ask her about if you end up taking her to dinner."

"If, Mom," Luke said. "Just as long as you focus on the *if* in that sentence." He stood to take his plate to the sink and asked, "Do you have anything else planned for today?"

"I was hoping you could help me move the dressers in the White and Wildflower rooms."

Luke was glad his mom was behind him with her own plate because she couldn't see the involuntary eye roll. He had no idea why she was never satisfied with the furniture arrangement in the house. He tried to make his voice teasing as he said, "I meant do you have any place you need to be, not do you have any chores for me to do."

Gloria shrugged. "I've just... I've been looking at those rooms this week and I think it was a mistake to change the dressers."

Luke turned to her and gave an exaggerated bow. "Your wish is my command."

She knew he was only kidding, but Gloria still sort of wished he wouldn't make it sound as though she was always ordering him around. They went upstairs together as soon as lunch was cleared away. The first room they came to was the one Gloria had named the Wildflower Room.

A wooden sign hung on the door from a gold-colored chain. Gloria had painted the name and the flowers around it before Luke was born. It had been his bedroom his entire childhood. Sometime during middle school, he had begun to beg his mother to rename the room or at least refrain from calling it the Wildflower Room when any of his friends were around.

She forgot this bargain once when he was fourteen. Luke had been sitting at their kitchen table helping two boys with geometry homework. His mom put a neatly folded sweatshirt next to the textbooks and told him to take it up to his Wildflower bedroom as soon as they were done.

The other boys shrugged it off as one of those embarrassing things moms say. Luke went upstairs later that night with a permanent marker.

4

He turned all five of the bedroom signs around and relabeled them. He began by writing Luke's Room on the back of the Wildflower sign. The White Room became the Black Room, the Wish Room became the You Wish Room and the Willow Room became the Big Ugly Tree Room. On the room where his parents slept, he wrote Witch's Castle.

Luke's father had been furious and doled out a lengthy grounding. He made his son paint over the words on all the signs, starting with the Winter Room, and hang them properly when they were dry. Two days later, however, Luke came home from school to find that his mom had neatly stenciled over his paint job on one of the rooms. No one ever said anything about the change, but the words Luke's Room had remained facing out until he left for college.

He entered the room now knowing those words were still on the back of the flowery sign. He pulled the drawers out of the dresser to make it easier to move while his mom told him some of the things she had done during the week. He moved the dresser while explaining a few things he was doing at work. Gloria was attending a charity dinner the following night and she talked about that while he pulled the drawers out of the other dresser. They reminisced about Luke's father while he moved that second dresser and for a while afterward.

When Luke decided he needed to leave because he had a few chores to do at his own house, Gloria asked if she would see him at church in the morning.

"Mom," he said, "I'm always at church. Why don't you ask me what you really want to ask?"

"Fine. Will you try to duck out before I have a chance to introduce you to the young woman I mentioned earlier?"

Luke sighed even though he just asked her to say that. "I promise to be polite. But you should not expect anything to come of it."

"You never know," Gloria said as she opened the door for him. Then she frowned at her driveway. "Is there any sort of clause that says you can return that truck in a certain amount of time… maybe when someone else is working?"

"I don't want to return the truck, Mom. I told you I like it." He waved as he pulled the keys out of his pocket.

Gloria closed the door and watched through the window as he drove off. People had been taking advantage of Luke Foster most of his life and it drove his mother nuts. She spent his early school days replenishing supplies that classmates borrowed and never returned. Later he became known as the kid who could be counted on to help with homework. She didn't see nearly enough of him during high school because he was always giving someone a ride somewhere. And in college, she had to pay off his first girlfriend, a conniving young woman who had intended to marry Luke simply to gain access to his bank account.

Gloria really hoped Rebecca turned out to be the sort of person who would appreciate her boy and not the kind to try to sell him a truck he didn't want.

Chapter 2

The light blue shirt came out of the back of Luke's closet. He preferred to wear black, gray or navy… colors that felt more subtle. This shirt had been a gift from his mom though and she would appreciate seeing it in use. She noticed and told him how nice he looked in light blue as he took the seat next to her in the pew.

When she jumped up at the end, she reminded Luke not to run off. He made his way slowly to the rather large lobby where he spotted his mom next to Elaine Johnson. They had their heads bent in close conversation and kept glancing into the sanctuary, presumably in the direction of someone named Rebecca.

Luke turned his back to pretend to examine a painting on the wall. It was Mary holding a baby Jesus and was actually a beautiful work. Luke had never stood this close to it, had never noticed that the background was several shades of blue streaked together instead of mixed. He was lost in the lifelike eyes of the baby when a female voice said, "Excuse me."

Luke turned to face the woman who had approached without his noticing.

"Hi," she said.

"Hi," he answered uncertainly. A quick glance had told him that his mom was still halfway across the room with Mrs. Johnson. "Are you Rebecca?"

The woman kept looking over his shoulder, but her eyes wrinkled slightly at the question. "Rebecca who?"

"Um…" Luke wasn't sure what to say to this woman who was apparently not Rebecca. She seemed around his age and had strawberry blond hair almost to her elbows. Her skin was fair and covered in faint freckles. Her eyes were light blue like his shirt and still focused on someone or something behind him.

7

Her gaze found Luke suddenly and she flashed a smile that lit up her entire face. "So I saw you standing over here by yourself and thought I'd come over and say hello."

Luke glanced over his shoulder. There were quite a few people and he couldn't tell who or what kept calling her attention. "Okay," he said.

"My name is Summer Slough." Her eyes flicked briefly to the side. "And you are?"

"Luke Foster."

"Luke… um, have you… Have you been coming to St. Christopher's very long?"

"All my life. Or so I've been told. I only remember back to kindergarten or so." Luke couldn't figure out why this distracted person was trying to talk to him. He still felt he should try to hold up his side of the conversation.

"Me, too," she said. "I'm surprised we haven't, um…" Summer's eyes appeared to be following movement behind Luke. Then she sighed before looking at him. "So are you seeing anyone?"

Luke shook his head slowly. That was not a question he had expected.

"Do you live in Port Harris?" Summer asked.

"No, I grew up here, but I live in Hartford now."

"Really? Me, too. I mean, I live in Hartford. I've always lived in Hartford. Do you know Pops?"

"The pizza place?"

"Yeah. Do you want to meet me for dinner there sometime? Maybe even tonight?"

"Tonight? What time?" Luke thought he was beginning to understand what was happening. He assumed that Summer had been looking behind him at someone who had either dared her to ask him out or bet her that she wouldn't. He thought he should say yes in case the bet included getting him to say yes.

"Um, 6:30?" she suggested.

Luke nodded. "I can do that." He liked Pops. He wouldn't mind eating their pizza even if no one joined him. He doubted a dare would include actually going out with him.

Summer smiled a little nervously. She looked as though she hadn't expected him to agree. "Okay," she said. "6:30. Bye." She hurried past him out the door.

8

Luke turned to see his mother hurrying towards him from the other direction. "Who were you just talking to?"

"I don't know."

"What do you mean you don't know?"

"I mean she told me her name is Summer and that's all I know."

"That's it? She just came up and told you her name?"

"Pretty much. Have you noticed how the blue in this painting is actually different blues?"

"It's very nice," Gloria said without looking at the painting. "So anyway, I have some bad news. Apparently, Rebecca Hilson just got engaged."

"I would think that would be good news for her."

"Yeah, yeah… good for her," she said. "Elaine and her husband are having lunch with the Lambs and they invited us to join them."

"Us?"

"You don't want to eat with your dear mother?" Her expression was full of feigned sadness.

Luke ignored it. "Eating with you is one thing, eating with a whole group of old people is something else. I'll beg off this time."

"Okay. But I'll see you at the house next Saturday?"

"Of course, Mom. Try to only want light things moved this time."

"Don't be ridiculous, Luke." She smiled knowingly. "I can move the light things myself."

Luke snorted as he turned to leave.

He arrived at Pops just before 6:30. Summer wasn't anywhere in sight so he snagged a corner booth and told the server he wanted to wait a few minutes before ordering because he might be meeting someone. Luke tried to make it sound as though his plans were not yet fixed. He hoped it would be less obvious that he had been stood up that way. He had no idea that Summer had arrived before he did. She was standing by a side window, peeking in while talking on the phone to her best friend Emma.

"Emma, he's actually here."

"He's standing in front of you?"

"No, he's inside. He just sat down."

"Shouldn't you go in then?"

Summer turned away from the window and clutched her phone tightly. "I'm starting to think this was not such a good idea."

9

Emma's laugh came through the phone. "You should have realized that before you asked him out. I don't think you can stand him up just because you've come to your senses. What's he look like anyway?"

"Not bad I guess." Summer took another look through the corner of the window. Luke was absently moving the cheese and red pepper containers around the table. "I suppose I didn't really look at him at church. He's actually cute."

"So it might not be so bad," Emma said. "Just eat fast if he's boring."

"Okay, I'm going in. Later, Em." Summer stuffed the phone into her purple patchwork bag. She carried a lot of useless stuff in the bag she'd had since her sixteenth birthday. Somehow the phone usually managed to stay on top where she could find it. Summer took a deep breath as she approached the front door. Just before opening it, she glanced at her clothes. She had changed after church into jeans and a bright green blouse. Her left hand came up to smooth her hair as her right hand pulled on the door. She walked over to the booth Luke had picked and sat down before he realized she was there.

"Hi," she said. "I'm kind of surprised you're here."

"I, um, said I would be." He decided not to point out that he had also doubted her word.

"It's Luke, right?"

He nodded.

"And I think you said you moved to Hartford recently. When was that?"

"Not quite a year ago."

"Do you like it?"

"Do I like Hartford?"

"Yeah. Does it feel much different than Port Harris?"

Luke shrugged. "Not really. Quieter. Less traffic I guess."

"Hmm…" Summer seemed to be trying to think of another question.

Luke wondered if he should ask something. He felt awkward, but more like job interview awkward than first date awkward.

Someone came by and asked what they wanted to drink. She called Summer by name and gave her a tiny wink before asking what they wanted. Summer watched her walk away and kept her eyes on the door to the kitchen after the server had disappeared behind it. Then she smiled brightly as she turned back to Luke. "Where were we?" she asked.

"Well," he said, "if we're going to eat we should probably talk pizza."

10

"Right." Summer glanced at her menu, but didn't open it. "Their square pizza is awesome. Do you like it?"

"I haven't tried the square pizza, but I'm sure it's as good as the round ones."

"Okay, what should we get on it?"

Luke looked down at the list of toppings. He knew what he liked on a pizza as well as anyone else. He wanted to give Summer a chance to state a preference.

She said, "How do you feel about mushrooms?"

"Um, maybe."

"Scratch the mushrooms. How about sausage?"

Luke nodded. "Maybe sausage with black olives?"

"Hey, that sounds good. How hungry are you?"

"Medium?"

"Perfect." Summer pushed her menu to the edge of the table. Luke closed his and copied the movement. The server placed drinks on the table, took their order and their menus, and left Summer and Luke in slightly tense silence.

The restaurant wasn't very crowded. There were two families with young children in booths on the opposite side and a table in the middle was surrounded by five older men. When Luke turned back to Summer, she had one arm on the table and was twisting the ends of her hair through her fingers. Her eyes were cast down as though she was mesmerized by the motion.

She was very attractive, more girl-next-door than supermodel. Luke still had no idea how she ended up sitting across from him, but he decided that he was interested in finding out. Or at least getting her to talk some more. "I believe you told me this morning that you've always lived in Hartford. Right?"

"Yeah." Summer kept watching her hair for a moment. Luke was beginning to think he should try another topic when she dropped the blond lock and raised her gaze. "My mom grew up here, too, so I guess you could say I have pretty deep roots here."

Luke nodded. "And your dad?" he asked.

"He did, sort of… I mean, my stepdad did. I don't know very much about my real dad. Honestly, he doesn't even know I *exist*."

"Oh." That didn't sound like a first date or whatever this was topic. Luke backed up slightly. "How long has your stepdad been in the picture?"

11

Summer let out a fast breath. "That's a story. I can laugh about it now." She smiled as she said it so Luke believed her. "But, well, he was one of my teachers when I was in sixth grade. That's how my mom met him, like at an open house or something. They got married when I was in eighth grade. There was this girl in my class who had a crush on him and when she found out that he was marrying my mom… that he was going to be living with me… Oh, it was embarrassing. I was happy when I got to high school and people no longer pointed out my 'daddy' in the hallways."

"Ouch. That sounds rough."

"It was a little weird at home, too. I mean, he's a nice guy and I could tell my mom was happy so I never hated him or anything like that. But I was used to calling him Mr. Morrison at school and my mom wanted me to call him Kyle. He said I could call him whatever I wanted as long as it wasn't mean." She flashed another smile at the memory. "I still can't really get used to it. They've been married about ten years and I've spent most of that time trying not to call him anything directly. When I'm talking to my mom I'll say 'your husband' and she'll say 'he has a name.'"

Summer paused for a sip of her water. She almost choked on it when Luke said, "My dad died."

"Um, recently?" she asked.

Luke shook his head. "Not really. I…" He stopped to figure out how to recover. People were always giving him a hard time about how he changed subjects. The startled look on Summer's face probably meant he had been too abrupt. He tried again. "You told me a little about your parents so I thought I should tell you about mine. I grew up with both of them, but Dad passed away almost two years ago."

"What happened to him?"

"Heart attack."

"He must have been kind of young."

"Not really. He was almost seventy-three and he'd had blood pressure problems for a while. It was still a bit of a shock. Mom's younger so I hope to have her around for a long time still."

"How much younger?" Summer asked. She appeared genuinely interested and it felt to Luke as though he had her full attention for the first time since meeting her.

"Promise not to raise your eyebrows too much?"

Summer nodded.

"She's fifty-two now."

Summer's hand immediately covered her forehead. "As far as you know my eyebrows are right where they're supposed to be," she said.

Luke grinned. "I'm not sure I believe you."

"How old were they when they got married?"

"You better keep your hand there. Dad was forty-three and Mom was twenty-one."

"Wow." Summer put her hand down and made her face serious. "I mean, that's a little unusual."

"I bet I know what you're thinking now," Luke said.

"I'm not thinking anything."

"Okay, but just for the record I'll say that they were married almost five years before I came along and I'm an only child."

"Okay, also for the record let me say that even if I had been thinking that, I would not have asked."

Luke's eyes met Summer's for a moment. "Now I believe you," he said.

Summer broke the connection and started fiddling with her silverware. She hadn't noticed that Luke had been watching her mouth until his eyes lifted a notch. There was something powerful yet indescribable in his direct gaze. She was trying to remember what they had been talking about when the pizza arrived.

"Wow, that smells good," Luke said.

Summer looked at the pizza. "One of the reasons I like the square ones is that the middle slices don't have that extra crust. Do you mind if I go straight for those?"

"No, I like the crust. I'll grab these two on the edge so you can get to the middle easier."

"Thanks."

The comfortable silence of two people very much enjoying their dinner settled over the table. Summer had almost finished her first slice when she restarted the conversation. "You were talking about your parents' age difference before. Did you get rude comments about that or anything that made it weird for you?"

"Sort of." Luke took another bite while he appeared to be thinking about what to say. "I didn't know that it was... unusual when I was a kid. I don't know, I guess it felt like all grownups were just varying degrees of old."

Summer nodded that she understood the perception.

13

Luke continued, "But then sometime around high school, the numbers meant more to me and I realized that Mom had been kind of young. It didn't help that she looked even younger. People sometimes assumed that she had been a teenager when I was born and when they saw that my dad looked like their grandfathers... Well, there were a few unflattering questions or comments thrown my way. But even then, I could see that my parents were happy together so it didn't matter so much."

"That's good," Summer said. "I mean, I'm glad they were happy. I knew this girl when I was in ninth grade and I went to her house a few times and her parents were *always* yelling. It was... I think even her stuffed animals were tense. She moved away before we really got close so I don't know what happened to her, or her parents."

Luke tried to look sympathetic and it wasn't difficult. His parents only disagreed occasionally and he hadn't wanted to be around when it happened. He didn't even want to think about what it might be like to live with constant arguing. "I think our next game is going to have a Medieval theme," he said.

Summer looked as though she was biting back a smile. "What game?"

"Yeah, my company... um, where I work... we make mobile games and we started one with like knights and princesses and stuff."

Summer glanced over her shoulder briefly. "What do the knights and princesses do?"

"Oh, well... we haven't really worked out the details so I'd hate to tell you something that might change." *Or that might bore you*, he added in his head.

"What's the name of the company you work for?"

"Game Smelters."

"Never heard of it. Is that in Port Harris?"

"No, it's in Hartford. Just a few blocks, um, that way." Luke pointed to his right. "It's right before Oak Street."

"Oh!" Summer's eyes widened. "Is that what's in the building with the weird purple stripe?"

"Yes, and that was there when we moved in."

"I know. The purple stripe has been there forever. The building has been empty for years and then we've seen lights on more recently. People in town have been wondering what sort of business was going to start there."

"We've been working almost since the lights came on. Our first game came out earlier in the summer."

"Why isn't there a sign?" Summer demanded in a tone that he couldn't be sure wasn't real annoyance. "Doesn't the boss know that people are curious?"

Luke laughed slightly at her indignation. There was also a bit of nervousness to his laughter. He didn't want to admit he *was* the boss. "We don't have a storefront since we sell our games online. We keep the doors locked."

"Still… a sign would be good. It'd make you, you know, more a part of the community," Summer said. And then she smiled mischievously. "And I already knew you keep the doors locked."

Luke narrowed his eyes at her earlobe. "Have you been trying to get in or something?"

Summer shook her head. "Not me, but someone I know. She tried to visit a few times under the guise of congratulating the business owner on the new venture just so she could get a peek inside."

"Wow. People are that curious?"

Summer laughed. "You are new to Hartford, aren't you?"

"I thought it was two lefts," Luke said.

Summer simply looked at him, waiting patiently for him to explain the new direction of the conversation.

"That's how new I am, or was. I actually got lost on my first trip to the grocery store."

"You got lost in Hartford?"

"Well, not entirely. From my house it's a left and then a right to the Hartford Market. The first time I thought it was two lefts so I turned the wrong way to go home and couldn't find my street. You can't go the wrong way here more than a minute before you're completely outside of town and that's when I realized my mistake."

"Can I get you anything else?" The server had appeared at the table and was anticipating an answer as she was poised to deposit the check on the table.

Luke shook his head and looked at Summer who said, "No, thanks."

The check was closer to Luke so he picked it up.

Summer grabbed for her bag at the same time. "Wait," she said, "I think I'm supposed to pay because it was my idea."

"Nope, I'm going to insist."

"Are you sure?"

He nodded.

When the check was picked up again, Summer said, "Excuse me a second," and jumped up.

Luke assumed she was headed to a restroom, but she cornered their server instead. The other woman shook her head and they exchanged a few words. Then Summer returned to the table somewhat out of sorts.

"Is everything all right?"

Summer sighed. "Do you want to do this again?"

"Okay."

"Hang on." Summer reached over and pulled her phone out of her bag. "I don't remember what days I work." She swiped her finger over the screen a few times before she looked up. "How about Thursday? Can you meet me here at 6:30 again?"

Luke nodded slowly. When Summer said "do this again" she might not have meant to ask him out. She possibly meant a repeat of the same confusing scenario that sometimes felt like a date and sometimes felt like he was distracting her from something else. But Luke was willing to try again to get to know her.

Chapter 3

"Summer's home!" Leo shouted as she came through the door.

"Summer will do the story," added Max.

Summer surveyed the scene she had just entered. Her stepdad, Kyle Morrison, was standing between her little brothers with a hopeful look on his face. Both boys had damp hair from their bath and were wearing jammies. Max's rocket jammies were tight around the middle and had legs that stopped well short of his ankles. Summer pointed at him and said, "Aren't those Leo's jammies?"

"It's okay," Leo said. "I told him he could wear them."

Kyle shrugged. "I couldn't find any bigger ones. We must be behind on laundry."

"I'm off tomorrow. I'll do a couple loads."

"Thanks, Summer. That would be great." He offered an ingratiating smile. "Now about that bedtime story?"

Max grabbed one of her hands and Leo pulled on the other one. They tried to lead her towards the stairs while spouting requests for what should be in the story. Summer smiled at Kyle. "Doesn't look like I have a choice."

Leo and Max were six and eight years old. The gap between her age and theirs made her relationship with them a little weird. She felt like part sister and part live-in nanny. Her mom and Kyle weren't taking advantage of her. She offered to babysit more often than they asked. Summer tried to make herself as helpful as possible so they would appreciate her still living at home rather than resent it.

She began working at the Hartford Market when she was sixteen and switched to full time after high school. At twenty-three and with years of responsible savings, Summer knew she could afford to live by herself. She didn't want to live by herself. She wanted to stay with this family until she could get married and have a family of her own.

After a story with dragons, airplanes, and Spider-Man, Summer went to her room across the hall and closed the door. Her mom met with other moms at the church on Sunday evenings. Summer didn't want to go downstairs with Kyle. He would have control of the remote and be watching something boring on the History Channel. She figured he could use a little alone time and she wanted to talk to Emma anyway. She plopped onto her bed and pulled out her phone.

"Hey, Summer. How'd it go?"

"He wasn't there."

"What do you mean he wasn't there? You told me you saw him sit down."

"No, Anthony wasn't there."

"Oh."

Summer could hear the disapproval in that short word. "What?" she asked.

"Well, I don't think seeing you with another guy was going to make him ask you out again anyway."

"Ugh. I wouldn't go out with him if he asked me."

Emma's throaty laugh came through the phone. "I don't get you, Summer. What was the point of making him jealous then?"

"He was such a jerk that I wanted him to see how little he affected me by how quickly I moved on. I found out his schedule and asked Luke to meet me there again on Thursday."

"What!? I thought you realized it was a bad idea."

"I was worried he might be boring or annoying or, I don't know... He turned out to be kind of sweet. Maybe a little goofy, but..."

"Yeah, I can see exactly how little Anthony affected you. Let me talk to my dear friend who knows that using someone is wrong."

Summer squirmed and began to fiddle with the handle on her bag. "It's not like I'm going to break any hearts with two dates. He won't even know."

"Your justification is that he won't know?"

"It's not justification. I think he had a good time anyway."

"You know what? I'm not going to say anything else about it. I'll just wait until your conscience kicks in. And I hope it's soon. Tell me about this Luke guy though. What makes you say he's goofy?"

"Well, he might be allergic to eye contact."

"Oh, no. You mean he was trying to look down your shirt the whole time?"

18

"No, nothing creepy. He just… he was always looking at other parts of my face or even the wall behind me instead of at my eyes." Summer remembered the moment she had noticed that, the moment he actually looked into her eyes. His were so intense. There was something about that moment, something she wasn't going to tell Emma.

"Maybe he was nervous," Emma said.

"He also did this thing where he would twist his plate every time he put a slice of pizza on it. And whenever he changed the subject, it was like he was already in the middle of a conversation without me."

"You mean he's bad at segues?"

"I mean I don't think he's ever been introduced to the concept."

Emma seemed to be smiling through the phone. "You don't sound annoyed though. Maybe you had a good time, too?"

"I did. You're not working tomorrow, are you?"

"I'm off until Wednesday."

"Great," Summer said. "You can come over and help me do laundry."

Luke smiled at the weird purple stripe as he unlocked his building on Monday morning. It started on the right side of the door and curved up before ending in a point on the corner of the building. He had been thinking about having it painted, but now that he knew the stripe was a fixture in the town it seemed a better idea to leave it alone.

He was the first to arrive, which was unusual. He went to his office and stood in the doorway enjoying the silence. There was an L-shaped desk in the corner facing out. He could see the backs of two monitors and there were several mobile devices stacked on a corner. The walls were a yellowy beige and there was a Lash LaRue poster hanging behind the desk. That had belonged to his father. On the opposite wall was a whiteboard that, instead of work notes, had a drawing of a man crying an actual river of tears next to a large number 5.

The 5 represented the number of days the interns would be working there before returning to school. They had started the countdown the previous Monday and were adding to the picture every time they changed the number. The man was supposed to be Luke after he no longer had interns in the office. Joey was the art intern and he was responsible for the picture. It had started just as Luke with a sad face, then the river began and it was winding its way through a distant town while various animals looked on in sympathy.

19

Nicolas and Lauren were the engineering interns. Lauren was also responsible for the picture. She told Joey what to draw. Nicolas got the honor of updating the countdown.

Though the whiteboard showed an impressive exaggeration, Luke would miss the three interns when they were gone. The office would be very quiet when it was again only him and Mike, the art director. All the other employees were contractors who came in for occasional meetings and otherwise worked from their homes.

Luke sighed and went to his desk. The wheels of his tall black chair rumbled across the plastic mat on the carpet before he sat down. He felt restless, but knew he should get started. He made a point of not checking work email on weekends so there would be a figurative stack of messages waiting. That seemed as good a place to start as any.

He heard a key in the lock just before 9 am. Mike had a predictable arrival because he came straight from dropping his older child at school. Lauren came in with him. She walked towards Luke's office and visibly startled when she saw him at his desk.

"I was waiting outside for Mike to let me in. I'd have knocked if I knew you were here already."

"Oh," Luke said. "Sorry about that."

Lauren felt her face get a bit warm. "Don't worry. I didn't knock so you didn't know. What are you doing here so early though?"

"I haven't been here that long and are you trying to imply that I'm normally late?"

"No." Lauren tried to smile, but he was smiling at her and that made her face stiff. "Just that you're normally later than I am."

Luke nodded. "Fair enough." His eyes moved from her shoulder to the whiteboard. "Did you spend all weekend thinking of things to add to the masterpiece?"

"I'm not telling."

"In that case, go pretend you have work to do."

"Yes, sir." Lauren backed up a few steps and went into the larger office next to Luke's.

Mike let Joey in only five minutes later. He also stopped at Luke's doorway. "Whoa! The boss is early," he said.

"Had to make sure the rest of you are actually getting here when you say you are."

Joey grinned and then joined Lauren next door. Luke sat at his desk bracing himself for Nicolas' arrival and comment. Luke rarely arrived past 10 am so he really wasn't that early. He was the last one in most days though instead of the first.

Nicolas appeared in the doorway as expected and said, "What are you doing here?"

"I work here," Luke answered.

Lauren's voice called from around the corner. "Leave him alone. We already told him how weird it is for him to be here early."

"Huh," Nicolas said, "it is kind of weird."

Luke sat down with his art director after lunch. They were in Mike's office, which had no farewell picture. Decisions still needed to be made regarding the new game.

"I think we need to reconsider keeping the card quests solo," Mike said.

"Why is that?"

"I think we need to play up the social aspects. Trading parts is arguably the most popular feature in Triangle Ships."

Luke nodded that he was listening. "But are you talking about keeping the quests turn-based?"

"Yeah. I think people could invite others to their quests and start it once everyone is on board. Then the time of the quest is shortened for each additional questee. But instead of everyone getting a reward, they would have to do an extra battle over that card. I think those battles would appeal to players because they wouldn't be risking anything from their decks."

"That makes sense. But do you think players would abandon the regular battles for the less risky ones?"

"Maybe in the beginning. I think once they had their decks built up though they'd want to prove it."

"Okay. Let's think about that and discuss it with everyone else at the Friday meeting."

"Sounds good," Mike said.

"I found a place that will print a sign for us if Joey draws one."

Mike laughed. "Have we discussed Joey making a sign?"

"Oh, sorry, no. I was thinking it might be nice to put a sign out front. Something simple that would let people in town know the name of the business behind the locked door. And you said Joey wasn't going to have a lot to do this last week."

"Okay, I'll text him in here." Mike pulled his phone out of his pocket as he spoke.

Luke said, "I could just tell him on my way back to my office."

Mike put his phone on the desk between them. "It's more fun to summon the peons."

"Enjoy it while you can," Joey said as he entered the room. "What's up, guys?"

Mike nodded towards Luke for the explanation. Luke stood and turned to Joey, who was a bit shorter. Joey was only around 5'6" and very thin. His hair was dark, thick and curly and his matching beard made him look older than twenty-one. The frames of his glasses were rather extreme rectangles that were almost black with a reddish tint. Every day he wore essentially the same thing... a white dress shirt, untucked, with jeans and a loosely knotted, outrageously patterned tie. "Joey, do you think you can design a sign for us?"

"A sign?" The hair and glasses didn't quite cover the worried expression that came over Joey's face. "You mean a sign for the front of the building?"

"Yeah. Just something simple that says Game Smelters."

"Possibly with a small ship in a corner," Mike interjected, "in honor of our first game?"

"Good idea," Luke said. "That might give people a hint of what we're up to in here."

Joey looked at Luke seriously. "Are you sure that's a job for an intern? That's like putting a face on your company."

"I know you have more artistic talent than I do so I'm not worried." Luke noticed that Joey was looking at Mike. He understood. "Why don't you draw three or four and let Mike pick one?"

Mike nodded. "Good plan."

"Okay," Joey said. "I'll get started." He smiled at both of them and left.

Luke followed only a few minutes later and could hear Lauren and Nicolas offering advice on the sign as he returned to his office. Knowing the project was in good hands left him free to focus on his own work for a few hours. All three interns appeared in his office shortly after 5 o'clock. Nicolas quietly changed the 5 to a 4. Joey and Lauren stood back to study the picture.

Joey said, "I really don't know if there's any way we can make him look sadder."

"I was thinking about that," Lauren said, "and I think we need to show something good coming out of the sadness."

"What do you mean?"

"Well…" Lauren used both hands to push her straight brown hair behind her ears. "It's like how we're all sad the summer is over, but glad to have the experience for our résumés." She glanced at Luke for a moment before adding, "And the glowing letters of recommendation. So even though Luke is sad that we're leaving, he's still happy he chose to hire interns and that should show up in the picture."

Joey arched his eyebrows. "You *have* been thinking about this."

Lauren bit her lip and turned away so they couldn't tell that she was blushing. She finished hurriedly. "So I think we should have the river flowing to where it's powering a hydroelectric plant."

Nicolas snorted.

Joey said, "I'm not sure I know what those look like enough to draw one."

"That's okay. We'll know what it is."

Joey got to work on the picture while his co-interns watched. Luke pretended not to notice them in his office at all. That was how it was supposed to work. They wanted to present the new countdown only after it was ready. Luke typed a little slower than usual while he half-listened to an argument over whether or not the building should have smoke coming out of it and whether that might actually be steam.

Lauren was nervous when she told Luke he could look. She hoped he would look at her first, but he didn't, not directly. He sort of nodded in her direction before taking in the updated whiteboard. "Only four days," he said in mock disbelief.

"I don't know what you're going to do without us," Joey said.

"I don't know how you're going to keep adding to that picture for even two more days. It's getting crowded up there."

Joey angled his head towards Lauren. "Ask her. She's the brains."

And then Luke did look at Lauren. His eyes locked on hers for exactly half a second before she had to examine her fingernail. She couldn't focus on it and her head buzzed. Luke had the most incredible eyes. They were an unusually dark shade of blue. When he looked right at her, Lauren was sure she could see some intense emotion, something like hope and vulnerability mixed together. His eyes gave him the appearance of a man who could love so deeply he would never recover from a broken heart. At least that's what Lauren believed. She knew she

23

might simply have a fabulous imagination or a fabulous crush. She did not, however, imagine how much her heart raced at the sight. "I'm sure we'll come up with something," she managed to say without raising her head.

"All right," Luke said with a quick wave. "You all have a good night."

The interns each gave some version of goodbye or goodnight as they left the office, repeating the sentiments at Mike's door as well.

Luke Foster left his office only a few minutes after his interns that Monday. He wanted to stop at the Market on the way home because he knew going home to find food would not be very effective. He was in the habit of picking up groceries on Saturday mornings before going to his mom's house for lunch. He had felt lazy that particular Saturday and intended to put off shopping until Sunday evening. But then Sunday evening he had had a date. He hadn't been expecting that. He still wasn't sure it really was a date.

The grocery store in Hartford was probably lucky that it was the only grocery store in Hartford. Its outward appearance was a bit off-putting. The paint on the sides was peeling so badly that it was more white-and-gray speckled than simply white. The large sign that said Hartford Market barely whimpered the words after what must have been many years of braving the elements. Its front doors opened automatically, but with a trigger in a mat rather than a motion sensor.

When Luke stepped on the mat, the door moved away from him on a hinge. He grabbed a cart and began to wander the aisles. Once inside, the store was more welcoming. It was clean, brightly lit, and the shelves were neatly stocked. Luke's favorite part was a small deli near the back. The premade options changed from week to week and were generally very good. And they all helped Luke avoid the chore of cooking for one.

He drew a steadying breath as he rounded the last corner and headed to the checkout. At the sight of the middle-aged woman with short chestnut hair, he let out the breath and felt his whole body relax. Luke had never seen this woman before. She wasn't Mabel. An older woman named Mabel was always there when he shopped on Saturdays. Luke was always as polite as he could be, but he felt that Mabel was a woman sorely in need of a lecture on privacy.

With this other woman, Luke was able to pay for his groceries without having to field personal questions or find out more than he needed to know about someone he didn't know. She understood that small talk was better.

Luke arrived at the office last on Tuesday to avoid more comments and consequently received several about how things were back to normal. A sign concept was waiting for his approval. Joey presented it while the others watched for Luke's reaction. He thought it was perfect and he told them so. The finished sign arrived on Wednesday afternoon along with two guys to install it. Luke signed off on the work and then invited everyone outside to appreciate it.

Joey really had done an excellent job. Instead of a spaceship in the corner, he drew several small ships within the letters. It was subtle, yet distinctive. And he had used a deep purple trim that matched the purple stripe and made that seem just a tiny bit less out of place.

The three interns went back into the building first. Luke was about to follow them when he heard a voice calling Mike's name. A sturdy woman with a tight gray bun was headed their way. It was Mabel, the woman from the Market. She hadn't called *his* name, yet it still felt as though it would be cowardly to duck into his building. Luke did it anyway. He locked the door, too. That was only out of habit and he cringed that Mike might think he locked him out on purpose. But he could hear Mike greeting Mabel and he had a key anyway. Luke went to his office to work.

It was nearly a half hour later when Mike entered. Luke was in the hallway getting himself a drink of water. He had forgotten that he left Mike trapped outside. Mike shook off a dazed expression and said only, "Well, Mabel likes our sign so the word is out now."

Luke nodded and they went to their respective desks.

The parade of interns happened to enter Luke's office while he was enjoying their work of art. They had added a row of old-fashioned lampposts to be powered by the new plant. "No peeking," Joey gently admonished as he picked up a dry erase marker.

Luke dutifully bowed his head over a page of notes. He was still aware of Lauren standing close to his desk in a pink dress. She had started the summer more casual. Only two or three weeks ago, she had started dressing up for work. There were a lot of reasons she might have decided to do that, but Luke hoped it wasn't an attempt to catch Joey's attention because Nicolas was the one who'd been noticing her all summer. In fact, he seemed particularly distracted at the moment.

25

Luke looked up when given permission and said, "Um, are you all coming in on Saturday?"

Joey looked at the countdown and then at Nicolas. "Come on, man, you only have one job."

"Sorry." Nicolas shrugged sheepishly and updated the number. Joey and Lauren had added rocks and rapids to the river to illustrate the faster flow.

"That looks great," Luke said. "I'm getting curious about what happens when you get to zero. Is there a grand finale?"

"The finale is that we leave," Joey said.

"That's the whole point of the countdown," Lauren added. "You are sad that we're leaving, right?"

"Of course." Luke gave an exaggerated sigh. "I'm crying that much on the inside. Now you all get out of here and have a good night." He waved.

Lauren was the last to leave Luke's office. She glanced back and saw his attention on his computer. She hadn't expected him to watch her leave. It was still disappointing when he didn't.

Luke planned to stay later than usual because he still had two letters of recommendation to write. Nicolas and Lauren worked hard over the summer and were very helpful. He was putting it off because he wasn't sure how to put that into a professional recommendation. He was only four years out of college himself and didn't feel fully qualified to write something so formal.

"Hey, I'm heading out," Mike said as he popped into Luke's office already carrying a laptop. "Let me just see the updates first." He came around the corner to view the whiteboard.

"Rapids today," Luke said.

"I see. It is going to be quiet around here next week."

"I know." Luke gestured to the picture. "We still have two more days though."

"Right. Bring on Thursday," Mike said as he waved and left.

Luke listened to the sound of the front door shutting behind Mike. Thursday. It was almost Thursday. He had spent so much time not thinking about Thursday that he wasn't sure it would ever arrive.

Chapter 4

Summer had to work on Thursday. She got off at 4 o'clock and went straight upstairs as soon as she got home so that she could take a shower. She tossed aside at least a half dozen outfits that were trying way too hard before she settled on a light blue shirt with white shorts and fairly strappy sandals. She dried her hair only partially and put it in two loose braids. She pulled out her phone, thinking she might call Emma. Then she put it away again.

She tossed the bag over her shoulder and stepped in front of her full-length mirror. Something wasn't right. Her bag thumped onto her bed as she made her way to her jewelry box. Summer typically wore jewelry only for church. She knew she had a silver and blue pendant that would look nice with her shirt. The pendant dangled just above her top button as she checked her reflection again. Pizza. She was going to have pizza and now she was trying too hard again. But it was already after 6 o'clock.

Summer picked up her bag and went downstairs. The boys were building something out of LEGOs and didn't notice she had entered the room. Her mother noticed. "Summer, you look nice. Are you going out?"

"Yeah."

"With Emma?" Her mother's tone indicated that she thought that unlikely.

Summer shook her head and mashed her lips together in a losing battle against the smile that wanted to plaster itself across her face.

Summer's mom, Megan Morrison, nodded her understanding. "Is this the guy you met at church?"

"Yes. His name is Luke."

Megan smiled. "I remember," she said. Luke's name had made its way into a few recent conversations. Summer hadn't intended to mention him to her family. She also hadn't intended for him to be on her mind during those conversations. She kept thinking about the way he tried to brush hair off his forehead when it was too short to be on his forehead. His dark blue eyes seemed to appear out of nowhere when she closed her light blue ones. And even the way he jumped ahead of her in the conversation was endearing. She was ready for another chance to keep up with him.

Kyle was coming home from work as Summer left the house. "You look nice, honey," he said. "Who's the lucky guy?"

"Luke," Summer said simply.

"Right... Luke..." Kyle paused with his foot on the first step to the porch. "We don't know much about this Luke guy yet, do we?"

Summer shook her head. "No... but I met him at church. That's a good sign, right?"

Kyle appeared to consider the information. "You're welcome to bring him by for dinner if you need help forming an opinion of him." He smiled, but he was only partially joking.

"I'll keep that in mind." Summer waved and turned to her car. She drove a slightly different way to Pops. Nothing could really be called the long way in Hartford, even if it wasn't the most direct route. She wanted to drive by the sign again.

It had caused a bit of a stir when Mabel returned after leaving for the day to report on the new addition to Main Street. She had apparently grabbed a local, Mike Fulcomb, and pumped him for information. The company made games, Mabel had said. She said it was started by a guy named Luke Foster who was relatively new to Hartford. Mabel guessed that this was the same Luke who typically did his shopping on Saturdays and was otherwise still a mystery to her.

She did get some details on his company though. Mike and Luke would usually be the only people in the office. There were other employees who worked from home and only one of them lived in Hartford. The others came from the city or even farther. Mabel was determined to find out more about the new guy. To her, putting up a sign meant that he intended to stay.

The sign meant something else to Summer. It had appeared only three days after she casually mentioned that she thought the business should have a sign. Was it possible that Luke had simply never considered putting up a sign or did her opinion actually matter to him? Even if it was a little of both, Summer was flattered.

She lucked into a parking spot right in front of the pizza place and straightened her shirt as she got out of the car. Luke was on the sidewalk only two buildings away. It would have felt rude not to wait for him, but standing still felt awkward.

Luke walked a bit faster when he realized Summer was waiting for him. He was glad to see that his memory wasn't playing tricks on him. She was as pretty as he remembered. With the red tint to her hair, the freckles he couldn't see from this far away and the eyes he knew were the lightest blue, she looked like a very colorful person washed out by perpetual sunshine. Or maybe it was only her name that made him think that.

"Hi, Summer," he said when he reached her. "How are you?"

She nodded a greeting. "Did you walk here?"

"Sort of. I came straight from work and it seemed pointless to move my truck two blocks."

Summer gave him a rather strange look, but didn't say anything.

"What's wrong?" he asked.

"Nothing. I... you don't look like a truck guy to me."

"Maybe I'm not. I just got it and it was kind of an impulse. But I don't regret it yet." Luke reached over and pulled the door open for her. Summer led them to the same booth as Sunday.

"This feels familiar," Luke said as he sat down. They were met with menus.

Summer left hers closed. "So what made you decide to get a truck?"

"It was different," he said.

"That's it?"

"Do you want the whole story?"

Summer nodded eagerly.

"Well, it was the first time I bought a car. My dad had a Camry that he let me drive in high school and he gave it to me when I left for college. I drove that car up until about two weeks ago. It had been having some problems and this time it was going to be an expensive fix so I decided it was time to let it go. I went to the dealership fully intending to buy a newer Camry because... well, because I guess I'm just that boring." He gave a slight smile. "I like consistency. But I got inside one to test drive it and all I could think was that it wasn't my dad's car. It just didn't feel right. There was this bright red pickup on the lot and it somehow struck me as the opposite and I wanted that instead."

Summer was listening. "That makes sense. Now that I know the story, you totally look like a truck guy."

29

Luke looked as though he was trying not to laugh. "I'm not sure what you just said makes any sense."

"Of course it does. Story matters."

"A story changes the way someone looks?"

"Yeah." Luke still had a doubtful expression so she tried to elaborate. "It's like how someone's personality can affect how attractive he is... or isn't." Summer didn't know if Luke was convinced or not because he dropped the subject as he noticed the server returning with drinks.

"What sort of pizza do you want?" he asked.

Summer lowered her eyes to the table. "Would you mind if we got the same as last time? It was really good."

"Didn't I just mention how I like consistency?"

Summer looked up. "That's right. You admitted to being boring so it's okay if I am."

Luke grinned. "I said I like consistency."

Summer also grinned. "I'm pretty sure you used the word boring before."

His eyes met hers only for an instant before he turned away to place their order. Summer felt her face flush. Luke noticed and tried to pretend he didn't. He was glad the evening was feeling more like a date than the last one. Nerves and all, he preferred this less distracted version of Summer.

"Did you see the sign?" Luke asked.

She nodded and bit her lip. Maybe he had put it up for her. "You know, when you told me the name of the company, I thought you said Games Melters."

"Oh." Luke let out a surprised laugh. "It never occurred to me that it might sound like that."

"Also, um, you said you worked there and I've since found out that you might actually be the boss."

"Where'd you hear that?"

"I'm not sure if I told you, but I work at the Market. It's kind of a hub of town info."

Luke could easily believe that. "I do work there and I would have told you I started the company if you had asked me to elaborate at all."

Summer felt a little guilty that she hadn't acted more interested before. Now she had a million questions. How had he started a company so young? Was he greatly in debt or at the mercy of investors? How many people worked for him? Was starting a company as scary for him as it

30

sounded to her? Before she could figure out if any of her questions weren't overly nosy, Luke said, "Mike got laid off."

Summer was confused. "Mike doesn't work for you anymore?"

"No, he does."

"Then what..."

"I thought you were going to ask me what made me start my own company."

"Oh, yeah. That's a good question. Let's pretend I asked that, but you have to back up I think."

"Okay." Luke took a moment to put together the story in his head. "I decided while I was in high school that I wanted my own company. I went to college and got a dual degree in engineering and business. Then I went to work for a games company in Port Harris. It sounds embarrassingly cocky now, but I only intended to work there for a year. I didn't think I'd know *everything*, but I thought I'd learn enough to go off on my own."

He stopped for a sip of water and to give Summer a chance to speed him up if she was losing interest. "And I ended up staying there for three years. Partly I realized that I had more to learn and partly I got comfortable. Other people were making the big decisions. Mike worked with me the last year that I was there. He and I became pretty tight and he's an artist which I knew I'd need if I had my own company. I had kind of put that dream on the back burner, but I was still thinking about it. Then there was a round of layoffs and Mike lost his job. That felt like God saying it was time to go for it. He, um, Mike has a wife and a couple of kids so I didn't know how he'd feel about leaving a job to work with me. Once he was in need of a job I was a bit bolder about asking him."

Summer said, "My dad, um, Kyle knows Mike some. I guess they went to high school together."

"Really? Mike's only ten years older than me."

"They were two or three years apart in school. Kyle is thirty-eight. My mom is forty-two if you're wondering. I know the guy is supposed to be older, right? Sometimes I think my mom feels funny about it. It's close enough that I don't think it's really a big deal."

"That's part of the reason I don't have siblings."

Summer smiled at him. It was like conversational whiplash, but she enjoyed it anyway. "What is part of the reason you don't have siblings?"

"My parents' age difference."

"How so?"

31

"Dad was afraid he'd die while Mom still had a bunch of kids at home. He was already pushing fifty when I was born and that happened to Mom's mom."

"She was left with little ones?"

"Yeah. Her husband – who was not much older, it was a car accident – died when my mom was only eight and she was the oldest of five."

"Oh, no. That must have been really hard for all of them."

"It sounds like things were fairly tight financially. Mom said they had some neighbors who helped out at first, but that she regularly babysat all four younger ones by the time she was twelve. They were a close family though. Mom still wanted to have more kids. Dad had other reasons for wanting to stop at one."

"What reasons?" Summer asked. It was a nosy question. Summer wanted to have lots of kids though and was feeling slightly indignant on behalf of the woman who was apparently talked out of her plan.

Luke brushed his hand across his forehead. "Dad and I were always pretty close," he said. "But it wasn't until I came home from college – his last year or so – that he sometimes started to tell me things… things I'm not sure he should have told me." He sighed and then connected his eyes to Summer's. "Aren't you tired of hearing me talk yet?"

"No," Summer said without thinking. She was lost in the expression in his eyes that seemed to say he would keep talking for as long as she wanted to listen. But his words sounded like a polite way of saying he wanted to talk about something else. She searched her brain for something to say about herself. "Did I tell you I have brothers?"

Luke looked surprised so she knew she hadn't before he shook his head.

"I guess technically half-brothers. My mom had two boys after she married Kyle. Max is eight and Leo is six. They're great, but they're so much younger than me that… I don't… sometimes I feel more like an aunt than a sister. Or maybe a cousin because I don't know what it feels like to be an aunt really. I'm not sure how to describe it."

Summer was rescued from the babbling by the arrival of a steaming pizza. Luke quickly grabbed an edge slice and used a napkin to turn the hot pan towards Summer.

"Thanks," she said as she scooped out a nice center slice.

Luke had his eyes closed so Summer did the same. She thought, *God, thanks for the yummy pizza. Please let this go well. I might like this guy a little bit.*

She looked at her pizza as she smiled to herself. Surely God would forgive what was more of an understatement than a lie.

A very catchy song was playing in the restaurant. Summer had not heard it before and she was caught up in trying to hear the lyrics when Luke said, "I think the lampposts are my favorite part."

"Favorite part of what?"

"The interns are drawing me a farewell picture on the whiteboard in my office. Tomorrow is their last day and they've been adding to the picture a little every day as they count down to the end. It's a picture of how sad I'll be when they go back to school."

"Um…" Summer flicked one of her braids back over her shoulder to keep it away from the pizza. She wasn't sure if the conversation had moved on without her already or not. "How do lampposts make you sad?" she asked.

Luke smiled around the pizza he was chewing. He swallowed and said, "It's this really crazy picture of me crying a river of tears that flows to a hydroelectric plant and that powers the lampposts."

"That's, um…" Summer let out a short laugh. "Do your interns do any actual work?"

"They've been great really. They haven't spent as much time on the picture as it might sound. I'm glad Mike suggested that we hire interns." Luke put down the unfinished slice and leaned in a bit. "Even better than the extra help is the feeling that maybe I'm helping them out, too. You know, relevant work experience before they finish school. Do I sound like I have a huge ego when I say that?"

"What? No."

"I don't sound as though I think I have a ton of wisdom to pass on at the ripe old age of twenty-six?"

"No, it makes you sound…" Summer was going to say sweet. That didn't sound like a professional word. "It makes you sound like a good boss."

Luke said, "Love triangles are definitely not in my skill set."

Summer covered her mouth with her napkin for a moment while she squelched what threatened to be a nasty case of giggles. Then she said, "Do you try to confuse me on purpose?" She immediately regretted saying it. Luke groaned and put his head in his hands. Apparently, he knew he sometimes confused people and was sensitive about it. Summer added, "It's okay. I just… I don't know if I should ask or if you'll explain if I'm patient."

33

When he lifted his head, Luke kept his eyes farther from hers than usual. They didn't leave the table as he said, "I don't know what's wrong with me. People are always telling me that I don't understand how a conversation works and I... I was *trying* to be normal."

"It's really okay," Summer insisted. "As far as quirks go, I think it's pretty likable."

"No, it isn't. Most people can't talk to me without constantly rolling their eyes. It isn't likable at all and I don't know how to stop."

Summer wasn't going to ask, but she thought she might have discovered what Luke had against eye contact. She wanted to get back to what had been a better than normal conversation. "You said something about love triangles," she prompted.

"Oh, yeah." Luke was still looking down and twisting his plate in circles on the table. "We were talking about my interns and their picture. I was thinking that while I'll miss them, the one reason I'm glad the summer is coming to an end is that there seemed to be a love triangle developing. That might have been awkward to be around."

"Only slightly less than being *in* one," Summer remarked knowingly.

"Really?" Luke stopped turning his plate and lifted his eyes to where they seemed to catch the necklace Summer was wearing. "Was that, um, a long time ago?" he asked.

"High school. It was our senior year and my friend Emma really liked this guy named Derek. She found out that he went to most of the girls' basketball games to watch his sister. So she talked me into going to a few games with her so we could sit near him and try to talk to him some. He ended up asking me out. Obviously I had to say no and that was awkward. And then I had to tell Emma and that was more awkward. And the thing is... I don't even really like basketball."

Luke laughed. Summer could tell his eyes were smiling again even though they refused to come anywhere near hers. He said, "Did things work out between you and Emma?"

"Yeah, we're still friends now. She was upset at first but she knew it wasn't my fault. She was the one who insisted I come with her to the games after all. As far as love triangles go, it could have been a lot worse."

Luke was nodding. He opened his mouth for a second, but then closed it quickly without saying anything.

Summer took a quick glance around the restaurant. Thinking about high school had made her remember Anthony. She was surprised to

34

realize that she was very glad he seemed to be staying in the kitchen. The place was fairly quiet and she hoped that he didn't even notice she was there. An elderly man was holding the door open for his wife, who Summer knew from the library.

"Want to hear something I think is funny?" she asked Luke.

"Yes, I do."

"Okay, it's about my little brothers. I don't know which one started it, but lately they've been using 'old lady' as some sort of all-purpose insult."

Luke scrunched his eyebrows together. "Why 'old lady?'"

"I have no idea. But that's partly why it's funny. They'll be fighting and one of them will be like, 'Stop it, you old lady,' and the other will say, 'Give it back, you old lady.' And there's just something about two little boys calling each other 'old lady' that makes me laugh."

"I like your laugh," Luke said.

That made Summer stop laughing and take a sip of cool water to try to keep her face from turning any more red. She thought she should simply say thanks and move on. Her thoughts were interrupted by a shrill ring from inside her purple bag. "Oh, no," she said. "I thought I turned that off." It seemed to take longer than usual to find the phone. She saw Emma's name as she pulled it out and silenced it.

"Is that important?" Luke asked.

"No, it's just Emma. I told you we were still friends. She was probably calling to see if I was home early."

"She wants to know what you think of me, huh?" Luke was eyeing the phone still in Summer's hand. "What are you going to tell her?"

Summer braced herself as she decided to say out loud the thought that occurred to her. "I'm going to say that I got your phone number?" She smiled hopefully.

Mild surprise showed on Luke's face as he recited the number. Summer dropped the phone back into her bag and zipped it. Then Luke said, "I don't understand why anyone needed to move the pretzels."

Summer put on a patient smile that she hoped wouldn't be mistaken for condescension while she taxed her memory for any mention of pretzels earlier in the evening.

"At the grocery store," Luke continued. "Three or four weeks ago they moved a bunch of stuff around and I just this last time figured out where they hid the pretzels."

"You could have asked someone."

35

"True. But it would still be annoying."

"*You* think it's annoying? I have to move the stuff. And people call me to ask where things are even when we haven't moved anything recently."

"People call you?"

"I mean at work. Sometimes they stick me at the customer service desk and it seems like half the calls are people inside the store wanting to know what aisle something is in."

"Do you know why they move things?"

"It's an attempt to keep people in the store longer."

"Does someone there enjoy watching people wander around?"

Summer leaned across the table and lowered her voice to a conspiratorial whisper. "It's an industry secret. When customers know where everything is, they tend to grab and dash. When they have to hunt, they usually end up finding more things to buy."

Luke nodded his understanding and also whispered, "It's still annoying." He was rewarded with an amused grin. Eye contact was more difficult than usual with such an appealing mouth in front of him.

Summer sat back against the booth. She was aware of where Luke's eyes rested. With a different guy, she might assume he was thinking about kissing her or that she had something in her teeth. With Luke, it might not mean anything. And she noticed that he hadn't requested her phone number in exchange for his. Then his eyes moved to the check that was sitting on the table. He had slid it to his side when the server put it down, but hadn't seemed in a hurry to leave. He pulled out a credit card and set it on top. Summer wondered if there might be a way to extend the evening.

"It's not too hot tonight," Luke said. "Would you be interested in taking a short walk?"

"Yes. Have you been around Hartford with a local yet?"

Luke shook his head. "You'll definitely need to show me the local places of interest."

The server grabbed the check and returned with a receipt shortly. Summer and Luke stood to leave and she was reaching back into the booth for her purple bag when a young man with heavily gelled blond hair approached. He was wearing a white apron and a red shirt with a Pops logo on the front.

Anthony stepped in front of Luke and said, "Hey, man, I hate to do this..." before Summer even realized he was there. She froze with the bag only halfway to her shoulder while she was sure her heart stood just as still.

"Do what?" Luke asked.

"Us guys have to stick together and that's why I need to warn you about this one," he jerked his head towards Summer. "She only brought you here to try to make me jealous."

Luke looked at Summer for a moment, looked right into her eyes and she knew he could see her guilt. She expected him to confront her, but he turned back to Anthony instead and said, "Did it work?"

Anthony blinked. "Did what work?"

"Did she make you feel as though maybe you were missing out on something precious?"

"No," Anthony snorted.

"Then you weren't paying attention and I don't know why you're worried about it."

"All right, man." Anthony put his hands up and began to walk away. "If you like being used, that's your problem."

Luke motioned for Summer to follow him and she did in silence. What could she say to make it right? Was Luke angry or hurt or both or maybe... neither? That was the scariest thought. Once they got to the sidewalk he said, "That's your car, right?"

Summer did not make a move towards it. "I, um... it is, but I thought we were going to take a walk."

"You don't have to," he said.

"I want to. It isn't like Anthony made it sound."

"That's okay," Luke said. "It's later than I thought anyway." He turned and began to walk away.

Summer watched for a minute. When he didn't look back, she turned to her own car in a daze.

Luke's truck felt a lot farther away than he had left it. He climbed behind the wheel and drove the half mile to his house. Friday was garbage day so he dragged the cart to the curb before closing the garage door for the night. It whined a little as he walked up the steps and then pushed his key into the lock. Once inside, he turned and slammed the door as hard as he could. He opened it wide and slammed it again. The empty house had nothing to say in reply.

37

Chapter 5

Summer sat in her car in front of her house waiting for the upstairs
light to turn off. She didn't want to go inside before Max and Leo were in
bed. She waited for a while even after she was sure they were. It was
twilight and a few fireflies briefly appeared and then vanished as she
walked up the porch steps and let herself in. Her mom was watching
something on TV and Kyle was sitting next to her with a book open in his
lap.

Megan Morrison smiled at her daughter. "How'd it go, honey?"

"Terrible," Summer said flatly.

Kyle closed his book. "Did he do something? Do I need to saddle
up the posse after this guy?"

Summer laughed in spite of her sour mood. "There will be no need
for a posse," she said. "*I'm* the one who screwed it up."

"Ahh." Kyle leaned over and kissed his wife on the check before he
stood up. "This sounds like girl talk then. I'll just take my book upstairs
to read."

Megan smiled slightly at his flight from the room. She turned off the
TV and looked at Summer. "Do you want to talk about it?"

"No," Summer said through a sigh. "Maybe." She sighed again. "I'm
just... I'm an idiot."

Megan sat patiently while Summer wrestled with how much she
wanted to say.

"I took Luke to Pops because Anthony works there. I wanted him to
see me with another guy."

"Oh? I thought you didn't like Anthony."

"I don't."

"Then why were you trying to make him jealous?"

"Mom, we covered that part. Because I'm an idiot."

"I see." Megan nodded even though she clearly did not see. "So I'm
guessing all this backfired somehow?"

38

Summer groaned. "Luke found out."

"How?"

"Anthony actually came out and told him. He said to watch out for me because I like to play games." Summer tried to sound like Anthony. "She only brought you here to make me jealous."

Summer's mom winced. "I bet that didn't go over well."

"That was the worst part. Luke defended me. He asked Anthony if it worked, if it made him feel like he let something precious get away."

"He referred to you as something precious?"

Summer held her pained expression and nodded slowly.

Megan said, "I think I like Luke."

"Mom, that's not helping. I like him, too. And now he's never going to want to see me again."

"Not necessarily. How were things going before Anthony intruded?"

"Great. I think. As far as I was concerned it was going well, but I don't know how to read Luke. I asked for his phone number and he gave it to me. He didn't ask for mine though. I don't know if he was waiting for me to offer or if he didn't expect to need it."

"Maybe he just assumed you'd send it to him."

"Maybe. I didn't though. And now… he'd want to give it back."

"See what you think tomorrow. Most things look better after a good night's sleep."

Summer looked as though she doubted that. She didn't argue with her mother though. She really didn't want to think about it. "What were you watching anyway?" Summer asked as she gestured to the TV. "You can put it back on."

Megan pushed the remote away from her on the couch. "No, there was something I wanted to talk to you about, too. Though I'm sorry you're already feeling down."

"Oh, great. You have more bad news?"

"It's about your dad."

Summer glanced at the stairs for a moment before she realized her mom meant her biological father, the one she knew only as a name. "What about him?"

"I looked him up again this week."

"I haven't changed my mind." Summer was adamant about not wanting to meet the man. She didn't want to complicate his life when there was nothing missing from hers. What she knew was that Megan met him her freshman year of college. He had dumped her before either

39

of them knew she was pregnant. Megan came home before she had the courage to tell him and had no plans to return to school. She had found more and more reasons not to tell him as the time and distance grew until she eventually left the decision to contact him or not with Summer.

"Okay," Megan said. "But you need to know... you can't now."

"What do you mean?"

"When I... I found his obituary."

"He died!?"

"A motorcycle accident. It was a few months ago already. I'm sorry."

Summer was trying to decide how she felt about the news when her mom asked her how she felt about it.

"I'm not sure. I'm as sad as I'd be to hear about anyone's death, but... he didn't mean anything to me. Is that terrible?"

Megan shook her head. "I only hope you won't change your mind and wish you had met him at some point later."

"I don't think I will." She looked at her mom. "Does it make you sad?"

"Not if you're okay."

"I am. Except that I feel like a lousy person for being more upset over my bad date than about a person's life."

"Guilt is powerful stuff."

Summer had to work early on Friday. It was the third early day in a row and she had had trouble sleeping. The light in the kitchen seemed incredibly bright as she stumbled around getting herself some cereal. Kyle was also up. He was a morning person. He knew Summer was not so he refrained from humming whenever he realized he was doing it.

The sun was rising as she drove to work. It would do no good though. The clouds were so thick no one could appreciate its rays. The day promised to be as gray as Summer's mood. She went outside briefly during a late morning break and it was still damp and drizzly. Even hidden, the sun was trying to make itself known by a heat that made Summer feel as though she was standing in steam.

In the early afternoon, the clouds finally opened up. Summer was nowhere near a window, but she could hear the rain pounding on the roof. Normally, she didn't mind her job so much. That day she felt stifled by it, almost to the point where she considered running outside to stand in the rain.

Summer made it through the day though and clocked out the same time as Mabel, whose hair was in a long thin braid and who was typically good for some cheering up. "Hey, hon," Mabel said as they began to walk out together. "You get the afternoon shift tomorrow, right?"

Summer nodded. That was a slightly cheerful thought. She could sleep in and then she had Sunday and Monday off.

"I hear the Casey boy is getting his cast off next week."

"I bet he's been dying to scratch something in there."

Mabel laughed. "Oh, yes. My oldest boy had a cast on his leg and he was always hollering about the itching. He stuck a pencil in there once to get at it and lost the thing."

"The pencil?"

"Yeah. The funny thing was the doctor didn't seem too surprised to find it in there when he took the cast off."

"I guess I'm lucky I've never broken anything," Summer said. "I sprained my wrist once, but I had a splint that I could take off."

"Shirley's chicken parmesan has been flying from the deli. I bet Hartford's new mystery man will grab some up. He's a fan of... oh! That reminds me; I heard you were actually having dinner with Luke last weekend. Are you getting friendly with the new guy?"

"That's none of your business." Summer's tone was harsher than she intended.

Mabel flushed. "Oh, hon, I'm sorry. I know I'm a talker. I don't mean to overstep."

"No, Mabel. I'm sorry I snapped. The truth is I really like him and things aren't going very well right now."

Mabel stopped and put her hand on Summer's shoulder. "First you pray... then you make him dinner. Guys can't resist a woman who can cook."

Mabel's advice was completely serious so Summer waited until she was alone in her car before she completely dismissed it. The prayer part was obvious. She had been chatting with God all day about how He could have let her do something so wrong. She was almost ready to admit that she had simply refused to listen.

The part about making Luke dinner was even less helpful. First she needed to figure out how to get him to talk to her. And cooking for him implied bringing him to the house with the rest of her family. Two little boys and two inquisitive parents would not make for a romantic evening.

Summer went upstairs as soon as she got home and took a shower. She hoped the hot water would help her relax. She pulled on some comfy pajamas even though she hadn't even had dinner yet. As she was pulling her hair into a soggy braid, she noticed a piece of paper on her dresser. Her mom had printed an obituary for Joshua M. McMurphy.

Summer let her eyes scan it tentatively. It listed his parents as survivors, but no wife or children. On the one hand, she was glad to see that. If there were siblings, she might have to debate about contacting them instead. On the other hand, Summer's romantic nature wanted a fairy tale wedding complete with happily ever after for everyone. Her mom had gotten that eventually and her dad probably deserved it, too.

The picture next to the words unnerved her slightly though. The only picture she had seen of Joshua was the one her mom gave her of a 19-year-old boy. He didn't look old enough to be anyone's dad and that made it easier for Summer not to think of him as one. This guy looked… almost fatherly. Summer picked up the picture for a closer look. His freckles were almost invisible in the black and white and he otherwise didn't resemble her at all. She stuffed the paper into a drawer. She had thought she was okay with the news the previous night. Now she just didn't want to think about it.

Max and Leo were sitting at the kitchen table doing homework when she came down. Leo said, "I'm making math mountains."

Summer would not have known what that meant if Max hadn't done the same thing when he was in first grade. "Excellent," she said. "Can I see?"

Leo pushed his paper to her side of the table.

"That's easy!" Max said. He pushed his homework in front of Summer as well. "I'm doing word problems. And they have two-digit numbers."

"You're both doing very well." Summer tried to keep her answer diplomatic. Neither boy needed his competitive streak encouraged.

Their mom came into the room then. "Summer, are you cooking tonight or am I?"

"Do you mind?"

Megan shook her head. "I know you have a lot on your mind. Have you talked to Luke?"

Summer only shook her head. Max and Leo appeared reabsorbed in their homework, but on the off chance Luke ever did come to their house she didn't want to risk the boys repeating something embarrassing.

42

Dinner turned out to be spaghetti, which was pretty simple. Summer regretted that she didn't at least boil some water for her mom, who had the table cleared before she realized that she didn't help with that either. She did pitch in when it was time to get the boys to bed. Her heart was not in telling a bedtime story though. Leo sat on his bed looking at her in disbelief, as though perhaps the super short story was only a trick, and Max tried to demand a better one. She tucked them in anyway and left the room amid moans of disappointment.

Kyle had brought some work home and was sitting at the table surrounded by stacks of papers. Summer sat across from him and watched. When he first moved in, their relationship had been helped along by this behind the scenes look at a teacher's life. She would sit and quietly watch him plan lessons or grade papers. Every now and then he'd ask her opinion on something from a student's perspective. It never felt as though he was trying to score points. It felt as though he really wanted her opinion. They had moved into a larger house after Max was born, but it was this same table they used to sit at and study each other.

Kyle must have been thinking about that, too, because he said, "It feels like it's been a while since you watched me work."

"No offense, but I kind of wish I had something better to do on a Friday night."

Kyle smiled. "Not my first choice for a Friday night either. But it frees up the weekend somewhat." He looked back at the paper in front of him and moved his hand down the page, pausing only once to mark a correction. The next paper had quite a few corrections. He frowned and rubbed a finger against his temple.

Summer spoke up before he began the next paper. "Did Mom tell you… did she tell you what happened last night?"

"On your date?" he asked tentatively.

Summer nodded.

"Yeah," he said slowly. "Was she not supposed to?"

"It's all right. Now you can tell me what to do without me having to repeat it."

"You want my advice?"

"It's not like I can ask my dad."

Kyle winced slightly as Summer recognized what she had said. She hadn't realized the obituary was still on her mind. Before she could finish kicking herself, Kyle said, "I know you'd like to see him again. I think regardless of if he wants to or not you'd still feel better if you apologized."

43

"I know you're right and I know that's what I need to do first. I just...How do I go from saying I'm sorry to finding out if there's hope for anything between us?"

Kyle appeared to consider her question. "I think," he said, "that if you tell him you'd like a chance to make it up to him that sort of implies you'd like to see him again. See how he reacts to that offer."

"That's not bad. But I'm still afraid of his answer. I'm afraid I found this great guy who doesn't want anything to do with me."

"I don't think he can be both."

"Both what?"

"I don't think he can be great *and* not want anything to do with you."

Summer smiled and tried to make up for her earlier gaffe. "That sounds suspiciously like something a dad would say."

"Well, I actually am *a* dad."

"Max and Leo are kind of lucky to have you."

Kyle acknowledged the sentiment with a tiny nod before moving to the next paper in his stack. Summer went upstairs to her bedroom before she kicked herself again. She should have included herself in the list of people lucky to have Kyle. He probably noticed the omission.

She dug her phone out of her bag. It was time to eat some crow with Emma.

"Hey, Summer," came her friend's cheerful greeting.

"I'm sorry."

"Um, why are you sorry?"

"I don't know yet, but I've been offending everyone I know today so I'm guessing it's only a matter of time before I call you fat and stupid."

Emma laughed. "I'll take my chances," she said. "How have you been offending everyone?"

Summer took a deep breath. "Let's see. There was the coworker I snapped at and the one I unintentionally ignored. Then I came home and offended the boys with my lame three-sentence bedtime story and then even when I was trying to be nice... I told Kyle that Max and Leo were lucky to have him."

"Oh, and not you."

"See... if you noticed it I know he did."

"Don't worry about it. I used to tell my dad I hated him all the time."

"I think this is different," Summer said. "I think, I mean I don't think I've ever told him..."

44

"He knows," Emma interrupted. "You don't have to get all mushy for him to know. How often do you tell your mom that you love her?"

"Actually, only when she says it first."

"See. Kyle knows you're not touchy-feely. But you know what I just realized?"

"What's that?"

"You did offend me."

"I did?" Summer asked skeptically. She could hear the playful tone in Emma's voice.

"You never called me back last night. How did things go with Luke?"

"It was a disaster."

"Really!? I thought you were starting to like him."

"It wasn't him. Anthony ruined it." Summer recounted again what Anthony said and Luke's response.

"Wow. He likes you."

Summer shook her head even though Emma couldn't see it. "I think he was just being gallant and showing me what *I* let get away in the process."

"I think if he does like you, even a little, then he'll give you a chance to explain."

"I hope you're right. I'm going to call him next. I just wanted to get some moral support first."

"Moral support I can do," Emma said. "I want things to work out with you and Luke so you can find out if he has any friends for me."

Summer rolled her eyes slightly, which made her think of Luke and the look on his face when he explained how most people handled his conversational skills. She vowed to try harder to keep her eyes in place whenever she talked to anyone. "Well," she said to Emma, "if I can get mushy on you for a second, I'll say that you are a very good friend for not saying 'I told you so' at any point in this conversation."

"Thanks. You'll let me know how it goes after you talk to him, right?"

"Of course."

Summer hung up and immediately found the newest name in her contact list. She stared at it until the screen faded to black. She closed her eyes and thought about Luke again, about the way she had felt when he complimented her laugh. She had to try. Her finger woke up the phone and called Luke's number before she could let her nerves stop it.

Voicemail.

She should have expected that. He wouldn't recognize her number. Or maybe he guessed it was her and didn't want to talk. She bit her lip hard as she worked her brain into a good message. "Hi, Luke," she said. "It's Summer. I need to apologize for the way things ended last night. I hope you'll let me make it up to you sometime. If you'll call me back we can make a plan. Or not, um... I could call again or... um, so I hope to hear from you. Bye."

Summer fell backwards onto her bed and let the phone drop next to her. She cast her eyes over the dots on her ceiling before she closed them. *God, I thought we were on the same page now. I was going to listen to You and You were going to help me make things right. Where was Your help during that lame message?*

Summer sighed and sat up. She texted Emma one word, voicemail, before she put the phone away. Emma would consider herself updated. She didn't need the gory, rambling details.

Chapter 6

Luke was happy that he missed the call from Summer. If he had seen the unknown local number flash on his phone he would have guessed it was Summer and been forced to make a difficult choice… the choice between feeling pathetic for wanting to hear her voice and feeling cowardly for wanting to let it ring.

Instead, he got to feel pathetic for listening to her message four times *and* cowardly for not calling her back. If he thought she really wanted to see him, he'd have jumped at the chance. But there was hesitation in the message that sounded as though she made the offer only to ease her conscience. He needed a day or two to patch up his ego before he'd be ready to help Summer feel better.

Luke was already in his truck when he remembered that he had intended to switch his shopping day to Monday. He decided to face Mabel's probing questions one more time rather than turn around. He ended up with a squeaky-wheeled cart that fought him as he worked his way around the store. The deli selection looked wonderful though. He grabbed food here and there and eventually turned his rickety cart towards the checkout.

Mabel looked delighted to see him. "Luke, honey, we're all so glad you decided to put up that sign. It brightens up the whole downtown."

Luke nodded. "They did a good job on it."

"Are you going to be hiring more people?"

"Not right now."

"Anna just goes on and on about how happy Mike is with you. That commute to Port Harris took so much of his time."

"I understand. I bought a house here so I wouldn't have to commute the other way."

Mabel nodded. "On Water Street, right?"

Luke wasn't surprised that the woman knew where he lived. She knew everything. He said nothing and focused on putting his last few items on the conveyor.

Mabel said, "The Yam Fest committee is still accepting floats for the parade. Do you think Game Smelters will sponsor one?"

"Um, maybe not this year." Luke had arrived in town just in time for Yam Fest the previous year. He had skipped the parade though and had no idea how a float celebrating yams should look.

"You should think about it."

He nodded to indicate that he had heard her, not that he was going to consider a yam float.

"I knew you'd go for this chicken parmesan. What would you like Shirley to make next week? I can tell her your favorites."

"I haven't found anything I didn't like yet."

"I never feel like I learn anything when I talk to you." Mabel sounded frustrated and Luke tried to cover his satisfaction. He was putting his bags back into the cart and sensing impending escape when Mabel said something that did surprise him. "I wish I could tell you what I know about Summer."

Luke paid for his food in silence. Did the whole town know that Summer was using him before he did? Was he the only one duped into believing she wanted to spend time with him? Mabel said something else about Yam Fest before offering a friendly farewell.

He dropped the groceries at his house and then headed out for lunch with his mother. She, at least, would be happy to see him. She gave him a quick hug as she met him at the front door and motioned him to follow her to the kitchen.

Gloria Foster was wearing a suit of soft brown with a long pleated skirt. She slipped a white ruffled apron over her head. It was spotless. She always wore an apron in the kitchen, but Luke couldn't remember the last time she got something on one. "Need any help?" he asked.

"Can you put the salad on the table?" She gestured to an etched glass bowl filled with spinach, strawberries and almond slivers. Luke carefully carried it to the next room, where two place settings were neatly arranged. His mom was pulling something out of the oven when he returned. He recognized her sausage casserole. It was one of his favorites.

"That looks great, Mom."

She smiled broadly as she carried it past him to the table. She knew it was one of his favorites. Her still white apron was folded and returned to its drawer before they sat down to bless their food and eat it.

Gloria could tell that something was bothering her son. She hoped it would come out with little or no probing. "How was your last week with the interns?" she asked.

"Fine. I'll never be able to use my whiteboard again, but I didn't use it much anyway."

"They kept up the silly countdown?"

"Yeah. It was fun."

"One of my kids graduated this week. He won't need me after the break."

"Good for him," Luke said. His mom was a regular volunteer at the closest elementary school. She worked with kids who were behind grade level in reading. If one of them caught up to his classmates, she called that graduation.

"I'll miss him though," she said. "He was a sweetie."

Luke sort of mumbled a response. His mouth was full and he didn't really have anything to say anyway. His mom always thought all the kids were sweet.

"I just got my invitation to the FCM charity ball. I don't suppose there's any chance I can talk you into being my escort." Gloria smiled hopefully.

"No way, Mom." She had talked him into going to a similar event shortly after his dad died. It was not an experience he wanted to repeat.

"Oh, honey, you look so handsome all dressed up. I never even get to see you in a suit for church."

"I'm still following your rules," he said. His mom insisted that appropriate clothes for church meant no jeans, no shorts and a shirt with a collar.

Gloria's face twisted slightly in frustration. "Those are rules for a child. A grown man should wear a suit to church."

"Mom, if I wear a suit to church people will think I'm an usher."

"Would that be so bad?"

Luke shrugged. "I'm not an usher."

"We could sign you up," she said with a wry smile.

Luke stared at his mother with one eyebrow raised.

She backed down and looked at her plate to stab a small piece of strawberry.

49

"What's the difference between a yam and a sweet potato?"

"Completely different plants as far as I know." Gloria watched her son for a moment. She still hadn't figured out what was on his mind. "Anything new with you this week?"

"Oh, um, we put a sign on the building."

"Really? It's about time. I'll have to come see it."

"You don't have to drive to Hartford to see the sign," Luke said. "I'll take a picture and send it to you."

"What if I want to visit you while I'm there?"

"Of course you'd be welcome." He reached for another serving of the casserole. "Was it blue?"

Gloria did not sigh. "Was what blue?"

"You used to serve this in a different pan. Wasn't it blue?"

"I think you're right," she said. "That one is larger. I've been making a smaller batch now that it's just the two of us."

Luke smiled wistfully. "I remember Dad liked it even more than I do."

"I'm hoping you'll help me with the beds after lunch today."

Luke put down his fork. "It's not bed day already, is it? I don't know why you still want me to help when you know you're just going to fix them and get annoyed with me."

"You'd think that after twenty-six years a person could learn how to make a bed. I shudder to think what your house looks like."

"Don't think about it," Luke said. In truth, his house was very neat and clean. Except for his bed. He refused to make his bed daily. He considered his mother a bit nuts where beds were concerned. Only two of the five bedrooms were in regular use when he was a kid, but about once a month they had what he called bed day. In addition to his and his parents' sheets, his mom washed the sheets from the three guest rooms. Then what seemed like every sheet in the house had to be ironed. Luke was tasked with remaking all the beds and helping to fold the other sheets. His mom would always work behind him grumbling about wrinkles and shoddy corners.

"Are you going to help me with the beds or not?" she asked.

"All right, Mom. If you promise not to freak out."

This time Gloria did sigh. She did not appreciate being accused of freaking out. She held her tongue and tried to think of a way to change the subject.

Luke said, "I like long hair."

50

It was a girl. She should have known. She hoped he was about to tell her something of this girl occupying his thoughts when he stood up with his empty plate. "You look done," he said. "Shall we clear this away so we can get to work on the beds?"

He said it with so much fake enthusiasm that it forced a laugh from his mom. She was glad his visit wasn't over yet. In fact, the sheets took so long that she was able to talk him into staying for dinner. Even after several more hours together though, she did not hear anything else about the girl. And she couldn't talk him into attending the charity event either.

Luke hit snooze one too many times Sunday morning and had to rush to get ready. He glanced at the two suits in his closet only long enough to reflect that he would not have put one on even if he wasn't in a hurry. He chose a plain navy shirt and khaki pants. The drive was uneventful and he arrived in plenty of time. His mom was saving him a seat anyway.

There was a reading about the prodigal son. Luke did not enjoy that story. God's forgiveness was of course a beautiful thing. The story made him squirm though because it made him feel like the other son, the one who stayed loyal and got no fatted calf. The only thing Luke knew about the other guy in his own story was that he had tried to humiliate Summer and yet she apparently preferred him. Luke wondered if she would appreciate the irony of having made the wrong guy jealous. No, he didn't particularly appreciate it either.

Luke extricated himself from his mom and her friends as quickly as he could and made his way to the lobby. He planned to go straight home. He passed the painting he had been examining when he met Summer. The blues somehow appeared more melancholy because of the association and that made him smile. Summer was right. Story did matter.

"Hey, stranger." A female voice made him jump. He turned to find a familiar and unexpected face.

"Nikki? What are you doing here?"

The woman had wavy nut brown hair that she shook back while she put on a playful smile. "That's some greeting," she said. "You don't sound pleased to see me."

"I, um, I'm just surprised. Are you in Port Harris for any specific reason?"

"What if I said I was here to see you?" She tapped a finger against his chest as she said you.

51

Luke took a very small step backwards. "I'd still be surprised. It's been, like, five years at least."

"I know." She tipped out her bottom lip slightly and put her hands on her hips. "That's a long time. And I thought we could talk. Are you free for lunch?"

"I am, but..." Luke tried to answer slowly. Curiosity and impatience were warring in his head. Curiosity won. "I guess we can talk."

Nikki smiled and tipped her head towards the exit just before they walked out together. That was the only part of the conversation that Gloria saw. She could not believe that horrible Nikki was back. Her hair had grown out, but it was definitely her. Was that why Luke had mentioned long hair? Were they seeing each other again? The fallout would be worse than last time if they were. Gloria went back into the church and pulled out a kneeler.

Luke's brief encounter with Nikki had more than one witness. Summer had been looking for him, hoping for a chance to say she was sorry in person. She saw the whole thing. She saw the woman in the strapless and completely-inappropriate-for-church sundress approach Luke. She saw the obvious flirting and she saw Luke leave with her. At that moment Summer felt worse than ever about her plan to make someone jealous. It wasn't a feeling anyone deserved.

Summer went home and sulked in between helping her mom plan meals for the week and pretending to be a dragon for Max and Leo to slay. After dinner she went upstairs and discovered that she had missed a call from Luke. She didn't waste any time dialing.

"Hi, Summer."

"Luke called me."

"He did?" Emma asked. "What did he say?"

"Nothing. I missed it and he didn't leave a message."

"Then why are you talking to me and not him?"

"I don't know. Should I call him right away even though he didn't ask me to call?"

"Don't over-think this, Summer. He called you and you want to talk to him. Call him back."

"Okay, but what if..."

"Just call him," Emma interrupted. "I'm hanging up now so you can call him. Bye."

Summer held the phone to her ear long enough to confirm that Emma was actually gone. She put the phone on the bed and stood there looking at it while she rubbed her hands on the sides of her legs. Waiting for Luke to call had made the weekend feel unbelievably long. All she had to do was pick up the phone now. It was time to find out if Luke could forgive her and start over.

She did three quick jumping jacks and then sat on the bed as she picked up her phone. She held her breath at the sound of ringing. "Summer?" he said as he answered.

"Hi, Luke. I... does this mean you're not angry anymore?"

"Yeah, I wasn't really... How are you?"

"I'm okay," she lied. He didn't need to know how miserable she was over seeing him with that other girl if he didn't want to see her anyway.

"Your message said something about, something that sounded like you might be willing to get together again."

Summer put her hand over her mouth for a moment while she composed her answer. "Yes, I would," she said.

Luke worked out some details and got off the phone quickly, *before* he messed up and said something off topic. He knew it was only guilt that made Summer accept, but he was going to take what he could get for the moment. After much more thought than should have been necessary, he came to a very simple conclusion. He liked her. He wanted to try to develop something between them no matter how things had started. Just because that something began as guilt didn't mean it had to end there.

Chapter 7

Monday was a very quiet day in the office, as was Tuesday. Luke left a bit early to take a walk down Main Street. He wanted to find a small gift for Summer. It had to be something less obvious than flowers because flowers were, well, obvious. And if he showed up with flowers, she would have to take them right away. He wanted something he could hold on to for an appropriate moment... if any moment felt appropriate.

Luke got his hair cut at a place right next to Game Smelters and otherwise hadn't paid a lot of attention to the other businesses on the street. He discovered on his walk that there were at least two other options for haircuts in addition to a bar across the street and an insurance company next to Pops. Beyond that was a place called "Things to Do." It appeared to be some sort of hobby shop and so far was his best bet.

He opened the door and resisted the urge to put his hands over his ears at the sound. A string on the door caused a length of pipe to clang against several differently-toned wind chimes all at once. It was about as musical as banging on random piano keys.

"One second," came a happy-sounding voice from somewhere in the small store. A woman who looked close to thirty came around a corner. She had short jet black hair with deep purple streaks and a gray shift dress over a pregnant belly. On her feet were shiny Mary Janes and yellow knee socks covered in pink bunnies. "Can I help you?" she asked.

Luke had no idea whether or not she could help him. He did know that he was not going to find a present for Summer in a bar. "Maybe," he said. "I'm hoping to find a present for someone."

"Okay." The woman put her hands on her hips and slowly looked Luke up and down. "Do *you* have a birthday coming up?" she asked.

"No." He did not ask what that had to do with anything.

"If you were an animal, what would you be?"

Luke stared at her at a loss for words. This woman was crazy.

54

She waved her hands as though brushing away the question. "All right," she said and fixed him with a serious look, "try this. What do you want the gift to say?"

"Ah, what do you mean?"

"Every gift has a message. Some are simple – like 'hope you have a nice birthday' – but I'm not getting that vibe for this one."

Luke thought about the question and decided to be as honest as possible. "I guess I want it to say something like 'Please give me a chance.'"

The woman nodded sincerely. "Right. This is for a girl and you don't know her very well yet?"

Luke nodded.

"Tricky," she said. "But not impossible. Follow me." The woman began to move slowly through the store with her hands out in front of her as though she might catch the perfect gift as it jumped off a shelf. Then she said, as much to herself as to Luke, "It can't be anything large or expensive. Those gifts say look at the gift. Smaller, more thoughtful things say look at the person giving the gift."

Luke worried that he had already been in the store too long. The crazy woman was making a little bit of sense. She stopped in front of a hodge-podge of items that Luke had trouble taking in all at once and she picked up a small book. It had red with gold trim on its hard cover and a jeweled clasp. "Has she mentioned keeping a journal at all?"

"No, but that is kind of pretty."

The woman frowned at him. "If she hasn't mentioned a journal, this would be a risk. To a woman who doesn't like to write, it might say 'I thought you might like some homework.'"

A small smile jumped to Luke's face. He would never have come up with that message. He was intrigued by the woman's thought process and began to hope that she could help.

"This can be a backup," she said as she put the book back on the shelf. She picked up something small and white. "Now this… won't work at all." She put it back and Luke saw that it was a ceramic turtle. "I know!" she exclaimed suddenly and grabbed something from a hook and handed it to Luke before walking away from him.

He was holding a plastic bag containing what must have been a thousand multi-colored beads, no more than two millimeters each. There was also a small coil of thin wire. Luke stood still waiting for the woman to come back and either explain why this gift would work or snatch it out of his hands. He had a feeling one was no less likely than the other.

She came back holding a few pieces of paper. "Now this will take a little time, but if you have the time, she'll definitely notice that you took the time and that will say, I think, exactly what you want."

Luke was still confused. "What do I do with this?"

"Oh!" She held the papers up for him to examine. "I printed these instructions for you. You can make a necklace or a bracelet. Both is too much." She paused to stress that important point. She did not continue until Luke nodded. "A bracelet can wrap two or three times and is simple, a necklace can be twisted – you'll need some sort of pliers to bend the wire – into a design like one of these." She showed him the second page that had pictures.

Luke felt unsure and in over his head, but this woman looked so positive that she had found the right gift that he didn't want to offend her by refusing it. He paid for the bag of beads and thanked her for her help.

Once he got it home the bag felt sort of juvenile, like a craft project for kids. He didn't have a better idea though and he didn't have to commit to giving it to Summer just because he tried to make one. The tiny beads proved tedious but after almost two hours he had something that, although not exactly like the picture, was a necklace. He found a small white box containing a few pairs of his dad's cufflinks. Luke had never worn cufflinks. He dumped them into a drawer and coiled the necklace into the box. It could sit there two more days while he decided if it was good enough.

Wednesday in the office was still quiet. Mike wasn't a big talker. They each kept to their respective offices and chatted virtually when questions arose. Luke hurried somewhat to be home by six, which was when he expected Zander to mow his lawn. The boy was pushing a mower from down the street as Luke pulled up. He got out of the truck and waited for him.

"Hi, Luke. Sorry I'm early."

Luke glanced at his watch. "Looks like we're both right on time."

Zander nodded and parked the mower.

"How's your first week of school going?"

The boy with sun-streaked blond hair and a prominent nose shrugged his skinny shoulders. "I know I'm supposed to hate it, but the summer felt so long it's almost good to be back. I know I'm going to miss the breaks though."

"Here's your money for today," Luke said as he handed Zander some cash. He understood about the breaks. The elementary and middle schools operated year-round with short breaks and the high school had a traditional calendar. Zander was a freshman.

"Thanks," he said.

Luke turned to go inside, but Zander stopped him.

"Hey, Luke? Aiden's grandma said you were making a float for Yam Fest. Do you need any help?"

Aiden was one of Zander's friends. He'd been mentioned before. Luke had no idea who his grandmother was, but he had a guess. Only one person had said anything to him about a yam float, though he was sure he had told her he was *not* going to be making one. "I don't think I'm doing a float," Luke said.

"Oh, all right." Zander appeared genuinely disappointed.

"What's the big deal with a float anyway?"

"The people who do the best float get to light the bonfire. That's the best part of Yam Fest."

"I guess I'll bring it up at a company meeting or something. If we decide to do a float, you can certainly help."

"Okay, cool. I better get to work." Zander reached down to start up the mower and Luke went into his house.

To get some more information on the topic, Luke stopped in Mike's office the next day. "There's a bonfire?" he asked as he sat across from Mike.

Mike narrowed his eyes in concentration. "You mean Yam Fest?"

"Yeah. The kid who mows my lawn wants to help us make a float because it has something to do with a bonfire. Do people get excited about this?"

An uncharacteristically broad smile appeared on Mike's face and wrinkled the corners of his eyes. "I can't believe it didn't occur to me that we could have a Game Smelters float."

"So you'd be excited about this?"

"We could do something so much better than Bennet Real Estate and I think they've won the most."

Mike was such an even-tempered guy that his eagerness was piquing Luke's interest. "Okay, explain this whole float and bonfire thing to me. Start at the beginning."

Mike pushed his chair forward and placed his hands on the desk between them. "Yam Fest goes from Friday afternoon to Sunday night. There's the usual street vendors and kiddie games and stuff most of the time. There's also a charity race sometime Saturday afternoon and some other stuff. The main events though are the parade and the bonfire. The parade is Saturday morning. They open the voting at noon and you only have an hour to vote for the float you think was best. They let the winning team know sometime Saturday evening and they get to light the bonfire Sunday night."

Luke stopped him for a moment. "All this just to light a fire?"

"You don't just light the fire, not unless you want to get booed. The idea is to make a skit out of lighting it or something fun to watch."

"A skit?"

"Yeah… or something. I remember one year a guy tried to light it with a flaming arrow. People freaked out that he was going to miss and well, I think that was the last year there was booing. Two years ago, they all dressed up in track suits with Olympic logos on the front and ran a torch through a long relay up to the fire. The best I think was this one group – people from the bank I think – they had one guy dress up like Frankenstein's monster and several others were chasing him with torches and pitchforks. That was awesome."

"Okay," Luke said. "What happens after they light the fire?"

"It's like a big town party. There's a stage on one side with an open mic. The acts range from awful to really pretty great. There's also baked goodies for sale, lots of sweet potato pie. We roast marshmallows over the fire and hot dogs and yams. I don't think anyone ever eats the yams though. They just burn them on purpose."

Luke found himself warming to the idea. It sounded like this float would make a lot of people happy. He wondered what Summer thought of Yam Fest. "Do you have an idea for a float?" he asked Mike. "I wouldn't have the first clue about making one."

Mike pressed his lips together and looked at the ceiling. "I'll have to think about it. Ours would have to be great."

"So you definitely want to do it?"

"Well, it's up to you of course. I don't know how much a float would cost, but I'll do most of the work if you're willing to back one."

They discussed work related topics briefly before Luke returned to his own desk where he did less work than usual. He would pick Summer up in only a few hours. Those hours went by surprisingly quickly as he was distracted by his float-inspired fact finding. He needed to find a trailer to rent and figure out what might be a reasonable budget for a float. He found pictures other townspeople had posted of prior year parades.

He went home long enough to clean up a bit and grab the present. It wasn't wrapped. He was afraid pretty paper might raise Summer's expectations too much. He put the box in the glove box as he got back in his truck.

Chapter 8

Summer's house was in an older section of town. There was no driveway and Luke parked on the street before walking up the sidewalk. It was about five minutes before six but Summer answered quickly. "Hi, Luke," she said with a big smile that quickly turned nervous. "Um, do you mind coming in to meet my mom?"

"No, that's all right." He stepped inside and Summer closed the door behind him. There was no entryway or foyer. He was immediately in the living room and it felt very full. Luke's living room had a large sofa, a recliner and a TV. That was pretty much it. This one had two sofas, two rocking chairs, lamps and end tables, a giant clock with shiny metal numbers on one wall and crayon drawings taped all over another. Various toys were scattered on the floor and heavy drapes hung around the windows. The TV had a game console with remotes and games scattered in front of it. And in the middle of the room two boys in matching blue and white striped shirts had stopped an imaginary sword fight. They were staring at Luke so he said, "Hello."

The older boy quietly said, "Hi," and then looked at the floor. The younger one ran to stand near his mother, who was coming from the kitchen, drying her hands on a towel.

"You must be Luke," she said as she approached.

"Yes, ma'am. Luke Foster."

"I'm Megan Morrison." She held out a hand to her visitor for a quick shake. "Where are you guys headed?" she asked.

Luke looked uncertainly at Summer. "Well, dinner," he said, "but we didn't settle on a place."

"Considering there are only two good places to eat in town and we've already been to Pops twice…" Summer trailed off and her mom nodded.

Luke said, "I'm afraid I still can't answer your question."

Summer laughed. "He's been in Hartford almost a year and you'd think he arrived yesterday."

60

"Well, I hope Summer takes you to the third best place to eat next time."

"I'll think about it, Mom," Summer said as her cheeks turned slightly pink. She turned to Luke. "Let's go before she gets any ideas."

Luke smiled politely at Summer's mom as he was gently pulled back through the door. He noticed that Summer took her hand off his arm as soon as they were on the porch. She wasn't sure what had made her touch him in the first place. She half expected him to recoil. She needed to redeem herself in his eyes, or at least try to explain, before she could hope for him to want to really date her. She was convinced that the night out was nothing more to him than a desire not to look petty.

"So what is the second best place to eat?" he asked her.

"Fred's. If that's okay with you."

"Is it okay with you if we make a stop first? I want to ask you a favor."

Summer agreed readily. She expected Luke to elaborate on the favor and instead he said, "What is your opinion of Yam Fest?"

"Oh, right. That's only three or four weeks away now, isn't it? What have you heard so far?"

"I heard I'm supposed to make a float."

Summer smiled at him as he opened his passenger door for her. "I hope you're not trying to ask for my help. I love Yam Fest, but I don't know the first thing about making a float."

"I don't either," Luke admitted. "But Mike is pretty excited and I can't let him do all the work."

Summer climbed into the truck and noticed that it smelled a little like Luke even before he got in with her. It was a light citrusy scent that made her take several deep breaths through her nose before she picked up the conversation again. "Do you have a theme for the float yet?"

"Mike has come up with one theme after another. I don't think he got any work done today after we talked about it. He hasn't decided which idea he likes best and he's waiting for me to..." Luke was going to say "give him a budget," but he always felt weird talking about money with someone who didn't know his situation. Actually, he just felt weird talking about money regardless of what the other person knew or didn't know about him. He finished the sentence with "...give him some input."

"I've actually never voted for a float before. I might make an exception this year if yours is worthy."

Luke tried to sound offended. "Are you suggesting my company's float might be anything less than spectacular?"

"I think *you* suggested it when you admitted to having no idea what you're doing."

"I'm a fast learner. And I happen to have a professional artist on my team… as well as the kid who mows my lawn so I'm not worried." Luke stopped the truck in front of his office.

"Are we going in?" Summer asked, a note of curiosity in her voice.

Luke nodded as he got out. Summer was already on the sidewalk when he came around so he walked up to the front door to unlock it. He pushed the door inward and motioned for Summer to go first.

"Mabel will be so jealous when I tell her I've seen the inside," she said as she stepped over the threshold into a fairly wide hallway with a water cooler and a narrow table on the right side. The table held a microwave and some snacks. She saw a mini refrigerator under the table.

"Go straight to the end of the hall," Luke said from behind her as he locked the door again. There were two small offices near the front that were empty and Mike's office was after that on the left. The conference room that had been used as an office for the interns was on the right just before Luke's office.

Summer entered it first and looked around. There was a framed picture on the desk of Luke with two people who must have been his parents. If Luke hadn't told her about the age difference, she might have guessed it was his mom and grandfather, or possibly his dad and his sister. The picture didn't appear that old, but Luke's hair was longer. She liked it both ways. Summer turned around as Luke followed her into the office and the whiteboard caught her eye. "Oh, that's the picture you were telling me about."

"That's actually what I want you to help me with."

Summer took a step closer. It was clear that much more artistic talent than she possessed had gone into the scene. "What do you want me to do?" she asked, clearly puzzled.

"Can you erase it for me?" he asked.

"What? I can't erase this beautiful picture."

"Someone has to because as great as it is, I'm getting sick of looking at it and I… they made *me* promise not to erase it."

Summer thought his frustration at keeping an insignificant promise was cute. "Are you sure you want me to do this?" she asked as she picked up the eraser.

"Yes, I already took a picture of it to save." His eyes hadn't left the whiteboard while they were discussing it and when they landed on Summer to reinforce the plea, she felt a flash of warmth and turned immediately to begin clearing the board. The evening was starting off almost too well. Summer knew she owed Luke a better apology and a motive, however inexcusable, for her behavior and she wanted to ask about that woman she'd seen at church. She hated to bring up any of that when they seemed to be getting along.

Luke felt much the same way. He wanted to know about the guy who had interrupted their last date. Was there an explanation that meant he wasn't competition or did Summer need more time to get over him? But bringing up another guy when Summer appeared to be enjoying his company was probably not the best idea. He watched her hand move across the whiteboard. Her nails were covered in a pale pink polish. She was wearing white shorts and a purple sleeveless shirt that matched some of the purples in her bag. Her long hair was loose on her back and the ends of it shook as she worked to erase the masterpiece. Luke had to resist the temptation to grab a handful of that hair. It looked so soft.

He wasn't paying attention to her progress and Summer turned around suddenly to catch him staring at the back of her head. She looked as though she had been about to say something. Whatever it was slipped away.

"I'd offer you a tour while you're here," Luke said, "except that you saw everything there is to see as you came in."

"Can you show me something you're working on?"

Luke glanced at his desk. "Well, not me personally because it doesn't do much yet, but there's some artwork for the new game in the conference room." He stepped into the hallway and Summer followed him to the next room. Roughly half of one wall was covered with drawings of people who might have popped out of fairy tales. Some of the pictures had a regal tone while others portrayed peasants. There were women with long gowns and pointy hats and knights in suits of armor with elaborately designed shields. A man in a monk's robe caught Summer's attention.

"Did Mike draw this one?" she asked.

Luke shook his head. "His intern did that one. Do you like it?"

Summer nodded solemnly. She thought it was a trick question because Luke was clearly the inspiration for the drawing. The friar had shaggy hair and a beard that Luke didn't have and he was much rounder.

The eyes, however, were a perfect match. If the drawing had been in color, they would have been a brilliant indigo.

"Really!?" Luke said seriously. "He creeps me out a bit."

"Did you tell the intern that?"

"I did. I was a little worried about offending him in case that wasn't what he was going for and he acted like it was the funniest thing he'd ever heard."

Summer started laughing. She couldn't help it. She couldn't figure out how he didn't see it. She laughed even harder when Luke tried to explain.

"Why is that funny?" he asked. "There's something about him that just... it's like he knows what I'm thinking or something."

After a moment to gain her composure, Summer held her hand over the bearded part of the monk's face. "You really don't see the resemblance?"

Luke squinted at the picture. "To who?"

"Come on! He looks exactly like you."

Luke studied the picture with a frown. Then he looked at Summer, more at the purple necklace she was wearing, before turning back to the monk. Finally he said, "Exactly like me, only creepier, right?"

"Of course." Summer was beginning to wonder if any guy could be *less* creepy than Luke. The pull she felt was definitely not away from him.

"What time do you have lunch?" Luke asked.

Summer tried to pretend the question was not sudden. "Depends on the day."

"I was thinking you're probably hungry. We should go."

"Okay." Summer led the way back out of the building. They left the truck where it was as the restaurant was right around the corner. It wasn't on Main Street. Luke knew where it was because he passed it to and from work most days. He had not yet been inside.

Chapter 9

Fred's Fine Food was painted in yellow block letters on a large window of a yellow brick building. It appeared well kept and fairly welcoming. The door jingled gently, as Luke thought doors should jingle, when they entered. A young woman with short dark hair made a sound higher than a greased piglet before she said, "Summer! I haven't seen you in ages."

She swooped in for a hug that Summer returned with one arm. "Hi, Missy."

"Table for two, huh?" The other woman gave Luke an appraising look before she motioned for the two of them to follow her. She wore no uniform or apron to indicate that she was an employee. She led them to a reddish brown booth in a row along the left wall. There was a stack of menus on a nearby table. She grabbed two and plopped them in front of Luke and Summer with a command to "pick something delicious" before she returned.

"I went to high school with her," Summer said to explain the earlier squeal. "We rarely talked then but she acts like we're really close whenever we see each other now."

Luke nodded and opened his menu. "What should I know about this place?"

"What do you mean?"

Luke shrugged. "I assume there's a local scoop on Fred's. Which foods are good, which recipe he stole from so-and-so... that sort of thing."

Summer smiled and leaned across the table. She whispered, "There is no Fred."

"Very funny."

She sat back and kept the smile right where it was. "I'm serious. Fred's is owned by a couple named Robert and Sue. I don't know if they couldn't decide which of them to name it after or if they just liked the alliteration."

Luke wasn't completely convinced that Summer wasn't pulling his leg. He decided to go with it anyway. "All right. What does the imaginary Fred make that's good?"

Summer opened her menu and began to point. "Let's see. Spaghetti and Meatballs is awesome. Grilled Ham & Cheese is pretty good. The Home-style Platter you don't want. The mashed potatoes it comes with are obviously boxed and well, it isn't bad it's just that most everything else is better. The Bacon Burger is also awesome. The Southwest Salad is good, too. If you get Fish & Chips you want..." She stopped abruptly when she glanced up and saw that Luke seemed amused.

"I guess you've been here a few times," he said.

"Were you paying attention?"

"When?"

"When I said there are only two good places to eat in Hartford."

Luke nodded his understanding. He still looked amused.

Missy came back then to take their orders. Luke asked for spaghetti because it was the first thing Summer had mentioned and he figured it jumped to her mind for a reason. Summer ordered the same.

There was a lull in the conversation after they handed over their menus. Summer unwrapped her silverware and began to ball up the paper that had held the napkin around it.

Luke said, "She never did explain."

"Who's she?" Summer asked.

Luke kicked himself, not for jumping into a topic but for the one on which he landed. He hadn't meant to talk about Nikki. She was on his mind only because he had seen her recently. It might not be pleasant but if he avoided the topic Summer would think he had something to hide. "Nikki," he said. "She didn't explain, well, anything really."

Summer didn't say anything. She was still trying to work the tiny piece of paper into an even smaller wad.

"Someone I used to know showed up unexpectedly on Sunday."

"Someone you used to know?" Summer tried to keep the suspicious note out of her voice, but it didn't respond to her plea. The memory of that woman flirting with Luke was stronger.

"We dated in college. It was years ago and I hadn't seen her since. Then she shows up at church saying she wanted to reconnect or something."

66

"Then what happened?" Summer asked. She was afraid she knew what had happened. They had gone out to reconnect. But then, why was Luke out with Summer instead?

"Well…" Luke hesitated. "Can I start at the beginning? I think… it might be better if…" Summer was just watching him squirm so he decided to tell it his way. "Her name is Nikki. We dated in college like I said, years ago and only for about two months. I was still trying to figure out if I even liked her. Sometimes it felt like she was a different person each time I saw her and I couldn't figure out which one was not an act. I probably would have given up except…"

He stopped and ran his hand through his hair. "This is embarrassing, but she seemed serious about me so I felt like I should, anyway…So one day I was supposed to meet her for dinner and she didn't show up. She didn't call or anything so I was worried. I went to her dorm and her roommate was there by herself. I asked if she had seen Nikki and she said she had just left. I asked her if Nikki was okay and she said she had seemed fine to her so then I wasn't worried but confused."

Summer dropped the teeny tiny ball of paper in her hand under the table. She thought of Nikki as she pressed the heel of her shoe into it. "And she didn't explain?"

Luke shook his head. "Not then or now. I tried calling a few times back then and didn't hear back. I saw her on campus occasionally and she'd turn around if she saw me coming or pretend I was invisible. That's why I had lunch with her Sunday when she asked. I thought maybe she was going to explain how I managed to offend her so badly that it changed everything."

"It wasn't you," Summer said with certainty.

"What makes you so sure?"

"I just am."

"I think you're right. Now. The lunch was weird. She was evasive about everything, even simple questions about what she's been up to the last five years."

It was clear in the way Luke talked about Nikki that Summer had nothing to fear from her. The time had come to make sure Luke knew the same about Anthony. "Luke, I want you to know that I'm sorry and that I never intended…"

He put his hand up. "You already apologized."

"To your voicemail," she mumbled.

"It's okay," Luke insisted. "You don't have to explain anything." He was curious. He was also suddenly afraid, too... afraid of hearing how Summer was so infatuated with the other guy that she hadn't been thinking straight.

Summer opened and closed her mouth a few times. It looked as though she might try to explain anyway when Missy appeared at the table with two plates of spaghetti. "Here you are, Summer... and Summer's friend."

She stood there for a moment looking between them before Summer realized she was hoping for an introduction. "Oh, um, Missy, this is Luke. Luke, Missy."

Luke said, "Hello, Missy."

Missy said, "Game Smelters, right?"

"Yes."

"You should know that your float has no chance against Fred's. We've been working on it for a month."

"How do you even know..."

"Oh, Mike's my cousin. He just called me to let me know about the competition." She used her fingers to make air quotes around the last word.

Luke was torn between wanting to support his friend and coworker and the fact that he didn't care all that much about the floats.

Summer jumped in with, "Oh, please. What's so great about Fred's float? I hear Jimmy's not going to juggle for you this year and he's the only reason you won last year."

"That's not the only reason we won. You just wait and see." Missy turned as if to walk away and then seemed to remember her job. "You have everything you need, right?"

They both nodded and Missy left.

Luke grinned at Summer. "I thought you were only a Yam Fest spectator."

"That's right. It's much easier to comment on other floats if you're not making one."

"I see. I never liked that song." Luke took a bite of a meatball and looked as though he approved.

Summer stared at him, watching for signs that he was going to elaborate without her having to ask what in the world he was talking about. Luke noticed the stare. For a moment, he appeared to be trying not to roll his eyes at himself. "I had a friend in middle school who ate at our house a lot. He used to sing On Top of Spaghetti whenever we had spaghetti. Now it always makes me think of the song."

"Hmm… that is kind of annoying."

"So there's no way I can talk you into helping with a float, huh?"

Summer watched as his eyes lifted slowly to meet hers. His passionate gaze was a secret weapon that could talk her into almost anything. Fortunately, it was a secret from Luke. Summer thought it might be best to keep it that way. She was trying to think of a coy response when Missy reappeared. "How is everything?" she asked.

"Good," Summer said.

Luke nodded. "Very good."

"How's Emma?" Missy asked as she motioned for Summer to slide over on the booth. She asked about Summer's little brothers as well and about how things were going at the Market. Then she made small talk with Luke, asking how long he'd been in Hartford and if he liked it so far. She didn't leave the table until Summer and Luke were both finished eating. "I'll be right back with the check," she said.

"Is it me or is it weird that she joined us?"

Summer sort of half-shrugged. She didn't want company on her date, but hadn't been surprised at all when Missy sat down. Mostly Summer was distracted by something that had happened while Missy was at the table. When Luke said that Hartford was growing on him, he stole a look in Summer's direction. It felt meaningful. It felt as though he did not think she was a horrible person. It felt like hope and hope was scary.

"Um, maybe…" Summer started, trying to swat away the sudden butterflies in her stomach, "maybe when we're done here we can take that walk we missed last week."

Luke nodded slowly. "Okay."

Missy returned with a check as promised and when she brought the receipt, she said, "Y'all be good tonight," and winked at Summer in a way that made her ears turn red.

When they got back outside, Luke asked which way they should go. Summer gave it some thought. "How about we go to the park?"

"I haven't been there so it'd be new anyway."

"Okay, this way." Summer pointed and began to walk.

Luke fell into step next to her. He thought about trying to take her hand. But even though she seemed to be enjoying herself, he still didn't know if she was friendly and guilt-ridden or if she saw the same potential he did. It felt like a good idea not to force her to pick a side yet. He kept his hands to himself.

Summer tried to entertain him with local color as they walked. "This is part of the parade route. It goes down Main Street and turns this way to end at the park. That house with the red shutters, Kyle's parents live there. The elementary school is down that way. They've added an addition since I was there. This house on the right, the woman who lives there dresses up as a witch for Halloween and sits on the porch with a cauldron full of dry ice. The kids all love it. Leo and Max were so impressed with the cauldron last year, they almost forgot to get the candy."

They followed a path around the park and Luke suggested they sit on the swings for a break. The sun hadn't really begun to set, but the shadows were long. Luke pushed himself back and forth a bit while keeping his feet on the ground. Summer wrapped her arms around the chains and twisted the swing to the side to face him. "I took Max and Leo here a lot over the summer so I was just on a swing a few weeks ago. How long has it been for you?"

"Probably years."

"I guess there aren't any kids in your life then? Do you have cousins?"

"I do. But they're not really kids and I'm not that close to any of them." Summer was watching as though she wanted him to keep talking. "My mom has four siblings. Three of them live out of state so I only see them once or twice a year. Her youngest brother, Rob, lives in Port Harris so I see him and his family a little more often. He has three kids, but they're all girls and the oldest is seven years younger than me so... not the best match for playmates."

"Right. My mom is an only child and my dad has one sister. I like her family okay, but the ages don't match up so well either. Her kids are 11, 12 and 15. Did your dad have siblings?"

Luke looked at the ground and answered slowly. "He does... I've never met them."

Summer sensed that was not due to them living far away.

Luke continued, "He had, has, um, two sisters... one older and one younger. They disagreed about some things and I guess Dad said his marrying Mom was the last straw for them. They refused to come to the wedding and he never saw either of them again."

"What did they have against your mom? Was it her age?"

70

Luke wasn't sure how to explain without revealing the thing about himself that Summer didn't know. All of the disagreements between his dad and his aunts revolved around the family money. They thought he should be more ostentatious, join a country club and drive a fancy car and basically show off. When he didn't, they apparently thought he should give his share to them so that it didn't "go to waste."

Luke knew that he only ever heard his dad's side of things, but it was difficult to imagine his aunts' rationale. After all, he grew up in a house with five bedrooms for only three people. It wasn't as though his dad didn't make himself comfortable. "Well," Luke eventually answered, "I suppose they just didn't think she was good enough for him."

Summer's face showed at least mild contempt for that idea. "Is that the other reason... you said before there were other reasons your dad wanted only one kid. Was his sisters' treatment one of them?"

Luke nodded. "He was hurt by the way they cut him off and didn't want to see his own children behave that way. They even sent back his Christmas cards."

"That's harsh." Summer picked up her feet and let her swing fall forward. Then she parked it again. "Would it freak you out if I told you that I wanted to have lots of kids?"

"How many is lots?" he asked.

"Not a boatload or anything. I mean like at least four... if I can."

"What makes you want a lot?" Luke sounded more curious than freaked out.

"A few things I guess. I never thought I was lonely when I was little, but now I see how much fun Max and Leo have and Emma has four siblings and they all get along great. I went to her family reunion with her last year and it was almost chaos with all the people, but it was a happy chaos. It seemed like someone was always laughing at something."

There was the most beautiful expression on Summer's face as she described her desire to have a large family. Luke found himself wanting to try to kiss her. He reached out for the closer chain on her swing and shortened the distance between them. Summer smiled and moved her hand to grab his chain as well. Then she looked suddenly nervous, as though she knew what he was thinking.

A nearby siren made her turn away. Luke watched as well as a fire truck went screaming past the park. He instinctively let go of Summer's swing to make a Sign of the Cross, a quick silent prayer for the emergency workers and those who needed them. He noticed the same movement to

71

his right. Summer smiled slightly at the commonality. The romantic moment was lost though.

She stood from her swing. "We should head back before the mosquitoes come out," she said.

Luke somewhat reluctantly began to follow her. He thought Summer looked relieved and wondered if he should also be grateful for the fire truck. Perhaps it had saved Summer from having to push him away.

They took a different path back to Luke's truck. Summer tried to tell him more about the town. She was distracted though. She was sure he had almost kissed her. The thought was thrilling and terrifying. She had been glad at the time that the siren provided an excuse to chicken out. Now she was trying to predict when she might get another chance while keeping up chatter about town dramas and who thought whose bushes were an eyesore.

When they reached his truck, Luke asked if she was ready for him to take her home.

"Do you want to come with me, maybe? The boys go to bed at 8 o'clock so they'll be asleep by the time we get there or at least out of the way. And my parents won't be... well, they're okay most of the time."

"They won't mind?"

"Please. My mom practically begged me to invite you to dinner. You know that's what she meant by the third best place to eat, right? They'll be happy."

"Okay. I'll come in for a little while."

"Great." Summer climbed into the truck feeling pretty good about her prospects. Surely if she walked him to the door afterwards... and if she was ready...

Luke moved to the driver's side feeling more convinced that Summer was only interested in being his friend. She wanted to go someplace with witnesses, someplace he wouldn't get any more romantic notions. Giving her the gift now would feel kind of pathetic. He tried not to think about how long it might end up sitting in his glove box.

"Why did she make it so loud?" he asked.

"I don't know. What was loud?"

Luke tried to smile. If he wasn't so disappointed, he'd have to admit that Summer would make a good friend. She had the patience for him. "Have you ever been to that store in town called 'Things to Do'?"

"Oh, a few times. But I still can't answer your question. It's been open three or four years and it's always had that thing on the door."

"What do you think of the woman… I don't know if she's the owner or an employee, but…"

"You mean Jill," Summer said. "She owns the place and she's funny. At first she comes off a little…"

"Crazy?" he interrupted.

"Um, let's say eccentric. But she's really very…"

"Crazy?"

Summer did have a pretty laugh. It was soft and not shrill or tittery. Luke enjoyed that sound.

"Stop it," Summer said. "Jill is actually known for being very insightful. Lots of people come from Port Harris or even farther to buy stuff they could get closer to home because she just knows people. I think that's *her* hobby."

"I don't know. When I went in there she… oh, no."

Chapter 10

Summer turned away from Luke to see what had distracted him. They had just turned onto her street and a police car with flashing lights was blocking the road ahead. Behind that they could see two fire trucks. They were alarmingly close to Summer's house. It couldn't be hers though. She hoped whoever's house it was got out okay.

Luke parked where he could and they began walking on the sidewalk. Quite a few people, neighbors and gawkers, were milling about and an officer appeared to be blocking the sidewalk as they got closer. Summer felt her chest tighten with fear as she saw a fireman emerge from her own house. She ran the last few paces to the policeman. "Is everyone okay? I live there. Where's my family?"

"What's your name?" he asked way too calmly.

"Summer Slough."

"Just a minute." He turned his back on them as he reached for a walkie.

Luke put his hand on Summer's shoulder. "It doesn't look too bad," he said. "No one's rushing and there's no ambulance here."

Summer was much paler than usual. "Maybe I'm too late."

"Has anyone called you?"

"Oh, I'm stupid," she said as she yanked her bag off her shoulder. "It was buzzing earlier and I ignored it." Summer got down on her knees and unzipped the bag. When her phone wasn't on top, she dumped its contents all over the sidewalk. Then she grabbed the phone from the pile. "I have a message from Kyle."

Luke began picking up the mess and putting everything back into Summer's bag while she worked frantically to hear the message. He was silently praying for her family. After a few moments, Summer relaxed visibly and put her other hand on the other side of her face. She closed her eyes. Luke had almost everything back in her bag when she returned her attention to him. "Thanks," she said. "They're fine. Kyle didn't give

74

me any details. He just said they're all fine and not to panic at the sight of the fire trucks. I'm gonna try to call my mom."

Luke nodded. Before Summer could make the call though, she saw her mom running up to them. She was calling Summer's name. The police officer motioned for them to go ahead past him. Luke stayed close to Summer as her mom pulled her into a tight hug. "Oh, I'm glad you're back," she said.

"What happened?"

"We had a pan of cocoa on the stove, a bedtime treat for the boys. They were helping me and one of them left a towel too close to the burner. Please don't tell them that though. I don't want them to feel responsible. It was my fault for not watching closer. I washed the sheets today and I went upstairs to remake their beds while the cocoa was heating up. Kyle was closed in our room because he had a phone conference with a parent. The boys were already running up the stairs to get me when the smoke detector went off. I couldn't believe how much smoke or how fast... we just had to get out."

"I'm glad you did."

Megan nodded. "If it was just me, I might have tried to put the fire out myself, but with little ones..." She put her hand up to wipe away a tear. "Anyway, it's out now. The firemen said most of the damage is in the kitchen. We'll be able to go in soon to collect some things, but I haven't figured out where we're going to stay tonight. I've made some calls, mostly so everyone knows we're okay and I got a few offers. No one really has room for all five of us though so I was thinking I could leave the boys with Kyle's parents and..."

"There's plenty of room at my house," Luke said suddenly. "I'll sleep on the couch and you can have the whole upstairs."

Megan turned to him with her head shaking slowly. Her face seemed to want to give a different answer. "We barely know you," she said. "We can't put you out like that."

"It would be no trouble. I've slept on that couch before just because I didn't feel like going upstairs. It's very comfortable and I love having guests. You should all be together after the scare."

Kyle walked over with the boys then and the smaller one wrapped his arms around his mom's legs. "Just for tonight," she whispered to Luke. Then she said more loudly to Kyle, "Luke is going to let us stay with him tonight."

Kyle didn't say anything as he could tell the decision had been made. He simply nodded.

"It's 116 Water Street. I'm going to run ahead to get a few things ready. You come over as soon as you're done here."

Luke received a few nods of understanding and Summer squeezed his hand for a moment as she said, "Thank you."

He could feel her touch lingering on his skin as he jogged back to his truck. Instead of going straight home, he drove to the Market. He had no idea what they might like for breakfast so he picked up several boxes of cereal, a tube of cinnamon rolls, eggs, bacon, and a box of frozen waffles. He also got orange juice and apple juice and some instant coffee. He didn't own a coffee maker and didn't immediately see one in the store.

Once home, Luke stripped his bed and gathered everything he might need into a suitcase. He put that near the downstairs bathroom and ran back up to put fresh sheets on his bed. He was grateful his mom wasn't there to point out a weird crease near the foot of the bed and more grateful that she had taught him to always have the guest bedroom ready.

He was standing in the hallway trying to decide if there was anything else to be done when he heard the doorbell. It was a welcome sound as he almost expected Summer's mom to change her mind. Luke opened the door wide for the family. He wanted to make a good impression on them. He had expected to be the one feeling vulnerable though and was slightly thrown by the reversal.

Megan came in first with an overflowing laundry basket in her arms. Kyle was right behind her carrying a black duffel bag with one of his sons clinging to his arm. Summer was also holding a small hand and a large bag. A strong odor of smoke entered with the family.

Luke pointed at the basket. "Can I take that for you?"

Megan held tight. "I've got it. If you could just show me where to put it."

"Of course. Follow me everyone." Luke led the way upstairs and gave a quick tour. "There's a bathroom right here and three bedrooms. The one on the end is completely empty so it might be a good place to toss stuff. This one and the next each have a king-sized bed. I have everything I need downstairs so you can spread out however you like. Do you need anything before I get out of your way?"

Kyle looked at his wife for a moment. "Unless you have a better idea, I'll go ahead and put the boys in here. I'll sleep with them and you and Summer can have the other bed."

76

Megan nodded. Kyle motioned for Leo to let go of Summer's hand and follow him. Then Megan turned to Luke. "Do you mind if… Everything we own smells like smoke. Is there any way we could use your laundry room?"

"Yeah, it's over here." Luke opened the door to a small room and peeked inside to make sure he hadn't left anything in there. "Help yourself," he said before going downstairs to give them privacy to settle in. He paced his living room while he heard the washer start up. It was nearly ten so his guests might choose to stay upstairs for the night. But he thought someone might come down for a while. Summer might come down.

Luke had left his kindle on the arm of his recliner. He sat and picked it up. He flipped it over in his hands a few times and then opened the cover to stare at an ad for a book that did not look remotely appealing to him. He closed the cover as Summer came down the stairs. Megan was right behind her. "Kyle will be down in a moment," she said as she took a seat on the couch.

Summer sat on the floor by the TV with her legs crossed. Luke watched her hair fall over her face as she looked down to trace lines in the plush tan carpeting with her finger. Kyle came and sat next to his wife before anyone said anything. Summer looked at the three of them and pushed her hair behind her ear. "So, um, what's the plan here?"

Megan sighed heavily. "I wish I knew exactly." She paused and looked at Luke. "Summer's like me, we don't like uncertainty. We always want to know what's going to happen next."

Kyle nudged his wife with a slight smile. He evidently knew that trait well.

Megan continued, "After I drop the boys at school tomorrow, I'm meeting the fire investigator and someone from the insurance company at the house. They should be able to tell us how long before we can go back home so I guess then I'll try to find a place for us to rent. I think this is the first time in my life I'm not satisfied with Hartford. It'd be really nice if there was a hotel within thirty miles."

"Please don't feel you have to rush out," Luke said.

"You're very sweet, but trust me, you want us out of here before the boys come home from school with all their pent up energy. And don't you have to go to work tomorrow? We can't stay here when you're not home."

"Well, we have a team meeting over lunch that I should probably go to, but I'll work from home the rest of the day and I could even Skype the meeting."

"I'll start making phone calls and hopefully figure something out before you have to leave."

Luke tried to nod in a way that showed he understood her desire to not be a burden without indicating they might actually be one. Summer described the damage to the kitchen and the weird feeling of packing up some belongings in a smokey house. Megan said she hoped they could get at least most of the smell out of the clothes. Kyle admitted that he had finished the conference and gotten distracted. He wished he had come downstairs sooner. Summer wished she had come home sooner instead of stalling at the park until she thought her brothers would be in bed. The fact that they had been in danger while she was deliberately avoiding them made her stomach clench uncomfortably. That was when she noticed how quiet Luke was. It would have been a brilliant time for him to jump them to some other topic.

Her mom was trying to hash out a few more details of the next day with Kyle, what she might want to pick up while she was at the house and if she should write notes to Max and Leo's teachers to let them know what happened. Summer wasn't listening. She was watching Luke, pretty much staring at him.

His eyes were cast slightly downward and it made him appear lost in thought as well as very attractive. She smiled to herself as she realized that if she hadn't let Anthony get to her, she probably would not have had the courage to approach Luke. Then again, maybe she would not have even noticed him. They had gone to the same church for years and she had never noticed him. How was it possibly that this amazing guy – someone who opened his home to her entire family in their time of need and made her laugh and made her blush with each eye contact – how had he been completely invisible to her?

Luke stood as he said, "I'll give you a quick tour so you can help yourself in the morning."

Summer blinked. "What?" she mumbled.

Luke wasn't talking to her though. Kyle followed him into the kitchen where Summer could tell from their discussion that Luke was showing Kyle how to find breakfast without waking him up. Kyle said goodnight when they returned and he headed up the stairs. Luke reclaimed his place in the light blue recliner.

78

"I won't be up much longer," Megan said. "I'm just waiting for the washer to finish so I can put our clothes in the dryer before I turn in."

Summer was glad to hear that. She had been up early for work and was starting to feel her eyelids droop. "I'll head up as soon as you do," she said. "I'd kind of like to sleep now, but I'm not sure I should leave the two of you alone."

Megan laughed. "Are you worried about me telling embarrassing stories or something? Because you know I can still do that with you in the room."

"I know," Summer said, "but at least I could make sure there are no exaggerations." The real reason she wasn't going upstairs was because she didn't think Luke would appreciate being left alone with her mom.

Megan gave her daughter a slight wink. "All right, if you don't want me to tell stories, I'll just interrogate Luke." She turned to her intended victim. "Summer tells me she met you at church. Is that right?"

"Yes." He glanced at Summer and the look said he didn't mind. He could say anything with those eyes.

"Have you been at St. Christopher's long?"

"Twenty-six years."

"Did you just answer two questions at once?"

"If you were going to ask how old I am."

Megan smiled. "You've never been in jail, have you?"

Luke shook his head seriously. He was pretty sure she was joking but thought it best not to take any chances.

Summer said, "Mom!" She did not seem to appreciate the joke.

"I hate to ask this, but I'm not sure Summer ever told me your last name."

"Mom, it's Foster," Summer interrupted. "I know I told you that."

"Did you? I guess I... Wait a minute! Are you related to Gloria Foster?"

"She's my mom."

"Oh, that's funny. I mean, I know your mom. If you were from Hartford, I'd have just assumed that I knew her so it's funny that I know her anyway. She was Max's religious ed. teacher last year."

"Really? What did he think of her?"

"He loved her. He actually told me at the end of the year that he wished she taught 3rd grade, too."

"I think she's actually going backward this year to 1st grade."

"Leo might be in her class then."

"Maybe. I know she's anxious for classes to start again. She misses the kids over the summer."

"Sounds like she's chomping at the bit for grandchildren. And you're an only child, right?"

"Mom." There was a warning in Summer's voice.

Megan turned to her daughter. "What? That's an innocent observation." But she looked at Luke expectantly.

"Yes, I know she'd love grandchildren. And yes, I suppose that falls entirely to me."

"And how do you feel about that because I know Summer…"

"Mom! Dial it back."

Megan smiled at Summer. "Just seeing how far you'd let me go. I'll behave. Luke, you work at that new company in town, right?"

"Yes. Game Smelters." He carefully separated the two words and peeked at Summer again. She felt her face get thoroughly hot and hoped her mom wasn't about to ask about the sign.

"Is that something you plan to do long term?" Megan asked.

"I hope so. Mobile games is, well, it's sort of hard to predict where it's headed." He paused for a moment. "The final spin is the loudest part."

"I think it is in ours, too," Summer said to her mother's confused expression. "The washing machine just kicked off."

"So it did. Are you still coming with me?" Megan stood and stretched briefly. Summer nodded and began to pick herself up from the floor. "Goodnight, Luke," Megan said. "Thanks again for letting us stay." She moved towards the steps without waiting for Summer.

"You're welcome and goodnight," Luke said. He stood as well. He felt as though he should even though it was a little awkwardly formal. "Goodnight, Summer," he added.

Summer thought about how she had hoped for a kiss at their parting for the night. She still wanted him to kiss her, but this goodnight was no longer the end of a date. The date had ended the moment she realized the flashing lights were in front of her house. She said, "Sleep well," and went upstairs.

Chapter 11

Luke couldn't sleep. The couch was as comfortable as he had claimed. It didn't help. He was worried he had unintentionally put Summer in a bad position. He wanted to ask her out again. What if this time instead of guilt she felt she had to accept because she owed him something? If her parents wondered about her sudden loss of interest, would she have to explain how she hadn't been interested in him in the first place? Luke knew he could help her avoid all that by simply not suggesting another date. But he wasn't sure he could help himself, not after that moment on the swings. There had been something in that moment worth chasing. Even if he only imagined it, Summer was still worth chasing.

He opened his eyes at a sound on the stairs and saw Summer tiptoeing down them. She was barefoot and wearing a T-shirt and shorts of pale pink plaid. Her hair was messy and falling in front of both her shoulders. Luke sat up as she reached the bottom stair. "Are you okay?" he asked. "Do you need something?"

Summer startled and immediately began pushing her hair back and trying to smooth it. "I'm so sorry. I thought I could get a bit of water without waking you."

"I wasn't asleep. Do you need help?"

Summer shook her head. Luke checked the clock as she went into the kitchen. It was nearly 2 am. He heard her open a few cabinets before she turned on the faucet. She returned to the living room a minute later and hesitated at the bottom of the stairs.

Luke gathered his blanket onto his lap to make room on the couch. "Do you want to sit for a while?" he asked.

She let go of the railing and walked over to him. She gathered her hair behind her as she sat and twisted it together in an attempt to keep it back.

"Can't sleep in a strange house?"

81

"Not exactly," she said. "My clothes smell like smoke and my hair smells like smoke just from walking through the house. Every time I move I smell it and it reminds me of *why* I'm sleeping in a strange house."

Luke had to restrain the impulse to lean over to smell her hair. He could smell the smoke from where he was. That didn't make the impulse any weaker.

"Why weren't you sleeping?" Summer asked.

He shrugged. "I'm not sure."

"Not as cool as you thought it would be to have a house full of strangers, huh?"

Luke smiled slightly, but didn't admit that had anything to do with his being restless. "Do you think everyone else is asleep?"

"My mom was up for a long time, but I'm pretty sure she was out when I came down. I don't know about the others."

"I hope they're comfortable at least."

Summer leaned forward suddenly and put her head in her hands.

"What's wrong?" Luke asked.

Summer talked to the floor. "Why do you have to be so nice and make me feel even worse?" She sighed and then sat up. "Can I tell you what happened with Anthony? It's really no excuse, but can I tell you anyway?"

Anthony must be the guy from Pops. Luke wasn't sure that he wanted to hear about him. He was curious though and Summer wanted to tell him. He nodded.

Summer squinted slightly as though she was thinking about exactly what to say. "So I knew Anthony a little in high school. Not much really. He was a year older and I guess I kind of had a crush on him, you know, back then. He moved away for college though and I pretty much forgot about him. Then he moved back to Hartford only a few months ago and started working at Pops. Someone in his family owns it. His great aunt, I think. Anyway, I saw him there a few times and thought he seemed sort of, I don't know, cocky. But when he asked me out I thought my teenage self would be mad at me for saying no and I figured it wouldn't hurt to try to get to know him better." She paused and glanced at Luke. He wasn't looking at her either, but was clearly listening.

She continued, "So we, he took me to somewhere in Port Harris for dinner. It was, well, not terrible, but we didn't click and it was short. He blared music in the car both ways so we really didn't talk much. Instead of taking me home though, he drove to his apartment and said I should

82

come inside for a bit. It was a, um, suggestive suggestion and I told him I would rather go home. He asked if I was some sort of prude. I just repeated that I preferred to go home. So he shrugged and said okay, but then he leaned over like he was going to kiss me, you know, *after* he insulted me. When I wouldn't let him he said that I was going to spend the rest of my life alone if I didn't loosen up."

Summer stopped talking to accommodate a large sigh. "I don't know what made me say it. But I just felt... I said that I wouldn't have any trouble finding someone else and that he'd be jealous when I did. He laughed. It was this nasty, dismissive laugh and that's when I got out of the car and walked home. He only lives a few blocks from me.

"That should have been the end of it and it probably would have been except that I saw him at church the next day. His parents go to St. Christopher's but I hadn't seen Anthony there once since he got back in town. Honestly, I don't think he even knew I was going to be there, but he gave me this look that made me feel like he was there just to laugh at me some more. And that's, well, that's when I saw you."

Summer had been talking to her hands and while she kept twisting them in her lap, she did make her head tilt a little bit closer to facing Luke. "It wasn't so much about making him jealous as it was about proving him wrong and I know that doesn't make it any better but it's... you should know that I don't..." Summer faltered in her explanation because she wanted to clarify that Anthony didn't mean anything to her, but saying it out loud implied that Luke cared, or that she believed Luke cared. She didn't want to say that before he did.

Luke said, "It is better."

"What do you mean?"

"Trying to make someone jealous sounds like manipulation, something you plotted. Your version sounds like you got angry and did something without thinking."

Summer knew that only explained the first time. She wasn't angry at the end of their first date. She had had a good time. In fact, it occurred to her that she might have used Anthony as an excuse to ask Luke out again without having to admit how much she liked him. She said, "Why are you willing to let me off the hook so easily?"

Luke shrugged. "I don't see the point in holding a grudge." He wanted to forgive her so that she would forgive herself. As long as she felt guilty, he'd assume that was why she kept hanging around. That and the debt she might feel after he sheltered her family might keep them

83

together just long enough for him to be completely devastated when she realized it wasn't enough. He tried to lighten the mood. "Maybe you should be upset with me for not letting you explain right away."

Summer picked up on the teasing tone. "It did take you two whole days to call me back, didn't it?" She pulled both her legs onto the couch and turned so that her back was to him.

"Do you think five minutes of silent treatment will be enough, or will you need to ignore me longer?"

"We might be looking at six minutes."

"Has it started yet because you don't seem to be ignoring me?"

"I'm trying, but you keep talking to me."

"I don't think you know how ignoring works."

Summer laughed through her sigh. Luke examined the thick mess of hair in front of him. The red tint was dulled in the dim light. He picked up a handful and pulled it to his face. "Your hair does smell a little like smoke," he said. Somehow on her it was a pleasant scent.

Summer stayed still and quiet. She wasn't ignoring him, could not ignore him. She'd always loved the feel of someone's hands in her hair. Even as an adult she'd sometimes ask her mom to braid it for her because it felt like pampering. But this was different. Luke's touch sent a new sort of shiver through her. He continued to comb his fingers through the ends of her hair. In the quiet darkness, the lovely sensation pulled her eyelids down and forced increasingly strong shivers.

"Are you cold?" Luke whispered.

She shook her head only a fraction, afraid he'd stop if she moved.

"Here." He took his hand out of her hair to push the end of the blanket from his lap onto hers. It was surprisingly warm.

Her "thanks" was nearly inaudible as she kept her back to him, hoping the interruption was brief. Luke returned his fingers to her hair. She closed her eyes again and felt the gentle tug on the ends. He moved his hand around and eventually found a stray lock by her ear. He pulled it back so that he could see the side of her face. "Aren't you ever going to turn around?" he asked.

Something in his voice said that he was enjoying the moment as much as she was and she was suddenly anxious. If she turned around he was going to kiss her and he would know. She was sure he would know that no one else ever had. It would be mortifying if she didn't know how to kiss him back. She sat paralyzed by the fear.

"Summer?" He let his hand drop.

Her head began to clear slightly. She turned back to face forward and tried to subtly put a few extra inches between them. She glanced his way with a mildly apologetic smile that she hoped looked more natural than it felt. "Sorry," she said. "I get distracted when someone plays with my hair."

"Me, too." His eyes were still lost in Summer's long hair, but they soon found their way to her mouth. He couldn't know how much emotion came through his eyes because they were completely giving him away. She could see how much he liked her and exactly what he planned to do next. As nervous as she was, Summer resolved not to move. If he was going to kiss her, then she was going to let him.

Luke noticed that she was uncomfortable and misinterpreted. She had just told him about a guy who tried to move too fast and now he had her sitting in his house in the middle of the night. They were sharing a blanket in the dark and he couldn't keep his hands to himself. No wonder she was squirming. She couldn't know he'd be content with only a kiss. He checked the clock as though he cared about the time. "We really should both try to get some sleep. Don't you think?"

Summer nodded slowly. "I guess." She pushed the blanket away and stood. "Um, goodnight again."

Luke waited until she was all the way up the stairs before he lay down again. He stared at the ceiling while trying not to wish Summer had insisted on staying longer. He must have fallen asleep at some point because he felt himself awakened by a whispered argument on the stairs.

"We're not supposed to wake him up."

"I know!"

"Stop talking then."

"You're the one who's being loud, you old lady!"

"You're the old lady. Now be quiet."

Luke kept his eyes closed so the boys wouldn't know he was awake. He sensed movement in the kitchen as well and assumed that was Kyle, who had said he was typically the first one up. The whispering got louder and more excited over the prospect of Lucky Charms and Luke congratulated himself on picking something they liked. After some moving chairs and sliding bowls, the kitchen quieted to muted crunching noises and a bit of humming.

He wanted to get cleaned up before Summer came down so Luke sat and folded up his blanket. Kyle noticed and said, "Good morning."

"Morning. Did you all sleep okay?"

The boys pretended to concentrate on their cereal. Kyle nodded. "I'm gonna go ahead and shower unless you need anything."

"We're fine, thanks."

Luke had never used his downstairs shower and it felt a little strange. It was effective nonetheless. He shaved and brushed his teeth and was about to leave the bathroom when he heard water in the pipes as someone turned on the upstairs shower. Summer's mom came down as Luke was finishing a bowl of cereal. Kyle left for work then. He had apparently gotten ready without Luke hearing.

Luke rarely started work so early, but Max and Leo still seemed a little afraid of him so he thought he should make himself as scarce as possible. He told Megan that he'd be in the den if she needed anything.

The desk was very neat, mostly because he didn't spend a lot of time there. The young boys started a lively conversation about their favorite cereals almost as soon as he left the table. He couldn't believe they were still eating.

Megan knocked lightly on his open door about an hour later to tell him she was taking the boys to school and that with all her errands she wouldn't be back until nearly lunchtime. Max and Leo came from behind her long enough to mumble an obviously scripted, "Thanks for letting us stay here," before they left for school.

Luke spent the morning *trying* to work. He didn't hear Summer come downstairs at all. The shower had turned on again so he knew she was awake. He wondered if she had found something to do or was simply staying out of his way. He would rather have simply given up trying to work to spend the time with Summer. He was afraid she'd feel bad for making him shirk. Around 11 am, when he was thinking that he really needed a break, the doorbell rang.

The front door was right outside the den. Summer came rushing by and said, "Don't get up," as she grabbed the handle to let her mom in. Luke kept his seat mostly out of surprise. Summer came from the next room and he wondered how long she had been downstairs without him knowing. He waved at Megan as Summer ushered her back to the living room and delayed his break to let them talk. He wasn't trying to eavesdrop, but they weren't trying to keep their voices low either.

Summer said, "Does the house look worse in the daylight?"

"Not really. They're pretty sure they will have it fixed up for us to move back in within a month."

"That's not so bad. Did you find a place for us to stay?"

86

Megan gave a rough sigh. "Almost. There's a house for rent on Walnut Street. Nancy Michaelson's mom used to live there and she just moved into an assisted living place in the city and they want to rent it furnished, which would be perfect because we wouldn't have to rent furniture separately. I got Nancy to show it to me and it has bunk beds. You know the boys would love that. The third bedroom doesn't have a bed for you, but we could figure something out. Or we could have, but Nancy wants us to commit to at least six months and preferably a year. But the insurance company won't pay for a longer lease than we need and I don't really blame Nancy for not wanting to find another renter right away. So I looked at another place – something George Kramer owns – and he's willing to rent short term but it's tiny. It's a one-bedroom apartment. We'd be so cramped. There are a couple of extended-stay hotels in the city. They're both on the west side though. We'd be forty minutes at least from school and the Market. It's not ideal. Neither is ideal. I need to talk it over with Kyle to see if we'd rather be squished or doing a lot of driving."

"It'd be easier if there were only four of you, wouldn't it?" Summer asked.

"What do you mean?"

"I mean, you'd be less squished if I moved out."

"Summer, this doesn't change anything. I know you don't want to live alone and you don't have to."

"Does your husband still think that?"

"He has a name."

"Yes, Mom. I know."

"He told me what you said the other day you know."

"What did I say?"

"You said Max and Leo were lucky he was their dad. We both know you meant that as a compliment, but..."

"But he noticed I left myself out?"

"Don't worry, he knows you still appreciate him even if you don't feel like his daughter."

"He's only fifteen years older than I am. I would think he'd be offended to have me call him Dad."

"He can't help the way he feels any more than you can. But regardless, you are a contributing member of our household and I don't think we should talk about changing that in the middle of this upheaval."

They were both quiet for a moment and Luke stood up to stretch his legs. He had a sudden idea and would need to make a stop on his way to the office. When he came around the corner, mother and daughter turned to him and he got the impression he had interrupted some whispering. He tried to pretend he didn't notice. "I guess I should go to work now. You both are welcome to stay while I'm gone."

"Nonsense." Megan stood quickly to punctuate the word. "I'm taking Summer to a nice long lunch at Fred's. Why don't you send her a quick text when you're back? Hopefully, we'll have plans by then and will only need to come here long enough to pack up our stuff."

"Let me get my bag." Summer ran up the stairs and down again quickly. Luke noticed that she had slipped on a pair of sandals as well. She was wearing a red sundress with big white buttons down the front. It seemed that she was wearing a different color every time he saw her and that she looked good in all of them. He was wearing gray with his jeans again. It probably looked as though he hadn't bothered to change clothes since yesterday. Summer smiled at him as they made their way to the front door. "I hope you were able to get some work done this morning."

Luke shrugged. "I got an earlier start than usual so that helped."

"Did that early start have anything to do with a pair of old ladies?"

"Sort of. I mean, they weren't bothering *me*. I thought I might traumatize them if I stayed in the same room any longer."

"They do need to warm up to new people," Megan said. "But you should enjoy it while you can. If they see you a few more times, they'll probably start demanding piggyback rides or something."

Luke smiled at the thought of seeing them more often because that would mean seeing Summer more often. He didn't say anything about that though. He simply waved to Summer and her mom as they went towards the street and he opened his garage.

Summer called, "See you soon," as she followed her mom to her silver minivan. She climbed into the passenger seat and tried not to be obvious about watching Luke entering his garage.

Megan gave her daughter a significant look as she started the van. "Will we be seeing more of him?"

"Well, we do have to come back to get our stuff."

"You know that's not what I meant."

"And you already know I like him. Stop trying to fish for details." Summer smiled at her mom. They were close, but there was still a limit on sharing. That's why she had tried to call Emma twice that morning. Emma finally returned the call as they were about to enter Fred's.

"It's Emma," Summer told her mom. "Order me a Coke and a Fiesta Salad. I'll be quick."

Megan nodded and went in alone.

"Emma, it's about time. Is it more embarrassing if I admit I'm clueless or wait until he figures that out on his own?"

"For crying out loud, Summer. You know I've heard about the fire by now. Shouldn't you start by assuring me that you're all okay?"

"I'm sure that you heard we're fine, too."

"Are you?"

"Yes. I suppose I'm technically homeless at the moment, but Mom's working on that. Nothing irreplaceable was damaged."

"Good to know. Where'd you stay last night?"

"Hey," Summer laughed. "There is a limit to your knowledge."

"So where'd you stay?"

Summer tried not to sound as though she had a grin stretched across her entire face. "Luke let us stay at his house."

"Really? All of you?"

"Yeah."

"I guess the date went pretty well then?"

"Well, it was kind of interrupted by the fire. But, yes, otherwise it was great."

Now Emma was laughing. "Great except that your house burned down? You must be completely gaga over this guy."

"I'm pathetic. You know what I did this morning?"

"What?"

"I watched him work."

"You what?"

"He was working at home and I peeked around the corner and just watched him sitting at his desk. Is that the saddest thing you've ever heard?"

"If I said yes you'd bring up that time I saved a guy's math homework. How long did you watch him?"

"I think it was only a few minutes. I was afraid he'd see me."

"That is a little sad. Does your initial question mean he hasn't kissed you yet?"

"No. I mean, he hasn't. I think he's waiting for some sort of signal from me that it's okay and I don't... I'm just afraid it will be bad because

I don't know what to do. Maybe I should have taken Jon up on his offer."

"No, you should not have," Emma said forcefully. "I did not want to see that." Jon was Emma's brother. He had found out about Summer's lack of experience about a year ago and offered to let her practice on him. She had thought he was joking, but Emma said later that she didn't think he was.

"All right. Just tell me what to do."

"Relax," Emma said.

"That's it?"

"Sorry. I think if you stop worrying everything will be fine."

"You're lucky my mom is waiting for me or I'd beg you to come up with something better."

"*You're* lucky your mom is waiting because I don't have anything better."

Summer gave a sigh into the phone before she put it away.

Chapter 12

Summer went into Fred's and found her mom sitting with a glass of water and untouched Coke. They had a pleasant chat over lunch interrupted by several phone calls. First Megan received a return call about a rental house in Hartford. It was no longer available. Then the insurance agent called to say he had found a house in Port Harris they could have for a month. It was only five minutes closer than the hotels though and they'd need to rent furniture.

The choices were not getting any better and Summer tried to convince her mom they should stay one more night with Luke. She was sure he wouldn't mind and surely something more fitting would be available if they put a few more hours into the search.

But then Megan got a call that made staying with Luke unnecessary. She thanked God for it. Summer got a text from Luke saying he was headed home again. She offered a similar prayer of appreciation. It was only by the grace of God that a nice guy had entered her life while she acted fully unworthy of one.

Megan insisted they wait a few minutes so it didn't look as though they'd been waiting on Luke. He was back in his den when they knocked on his door.

"How was lunch?" he asked.

"Great," Megan said. "We have a place to stay and we can pack up right now." She went up the stairs without another word so Summer shared the details.

"We're going to stay in town. There's a place on Walnut Street. The woman said at first that she didn't want to rent short term, but she called back to say she changed her mind. I guess she reconsidered because of the fire. I'm glad she was willing to make an exception because I think we'd have been in the city otherwise. Yes, I know it would have been temporary and a longish commute is not a terrible hardship. This is still better."

91

Luke smiled at her. "I'm glad you're happy. I would have hated to have you all accept something uncomfortable just to rush out of here."

"You really are too nice for your own good, you know. This is going to make Mom even more adamant about having you over for dinner, though we'll probably need a few days to get settled."

"What do you think of flying yams?"

"Flying yams?" Summer laughed. "Is that your float idea?"

Luke shook his head. "Mike was just talking about that. If it makes you laugh it must be as bad as I thought."

"Not necessarily. A float that makes people laugh might be memorable enough to get some votes."

"I don't know. There's memorable and then there's the bad kind of memorable."

"I've seen some pretty ridiculous floats. I doubt you're in danger of the bad kind of memorable," Summer said. She fidgeted with a button on her dress for a moment. "I think I should help my mom."

"Okay, but first... do you think maybe I could see you sometime over the weekend?"

Summer felt her face burn slightly under his hopeful expression. "Yeah," she said slowly. "I have to work tomorrow, but I get off at four. Maybe... maybe we could make dinner together, except that we'd have to do it here."

"That sounds fun." It did. Luke had discovered a perk to having only two good restaurants in town.

"I'll come over around five then?"

Luke nodded and Summer hurried off to help her mom before the giddy smile showed itself.

The house on Walnut Street was well received by its new inhabitants. Megan mostly marveled at how clean and clutter-free everything was and her boys loved that the sparse furnishings gave them more room to run around. Megan had to stop a game of indoor tag and something upstairs that sounded suspiciously like jumping off the top bunk.

Summer liked the window seat in what would be her bedroom. There was no bed in the room, but one was supposed to be delivered in a few days. They had stopped at their house for a few more supplies including an air mattress that would do until then. She volunteered to run to the Market rather than stay with her excited brothers.

Summer knew the aisles well and filled the cart with a few staples and a few simple meals. Mabel was at the register.

"Summer! Honey, I'm so glad to see you're okay."

"I wasn't even there."

"Still. Fires are scary things. The good Lord must have been watching over your family."

"And I'm grateful to Him."

"Nancy got you moved in already?"

Summer nodded. "It looks like a nice house. Just needs food." She glanced at the items Mabel was scanning.

"Nancy and I are pretty tight," Mabel said. "She was just busting to tell someone."

"Not a big deal. I assume everyone will know we're staying there soon."

"Right." Mabel appeared to concentrate on her work. There was something about her reaction that told Summer there was more to what Nancy had told her.

"Did Nancy tell you something else?"

Mabel looked guilty. "I can't say."

"You can't say or you don't want to say?"

"Both."

Summer didn't like the fact that Mabel seemed to know something that might have to do with her. And only something very significant would prompt Mabel to be secretive. "Can you give me a hint?" she asked.

Mabel shook her head. "He really didn't want any of you to know."

"He? I thought we were talking about Nancy."

"We are. Or we're not. We're talking about rain. I heard we're in for some tomorrow."

Summer paused to put a few bags back into her cart. "If you tell me this secret doesn't have anything to do with me then I'll let us talk about rain."

"Oh, hon, it's nothing bad. Let's just say I know why Nancy changed her mind about renting to your folks."

"I thought she felt bad about the fire. There was a reason that had to do with a *he?*"

Mabel pressed her lips together and shook her head.

"It must be Luke. He heard Mom tell me about the places she was looking at. How did he get Nancy to change her mind?"

93

"I can't say."

"Yes, you can. I promise not to tell my parents or anyone else."

Mabel shook her head again. She worked to scan the last few items a bit faster.

"Please tell me what you know, Mabel."

"That's $62.02."

Summer held up her credit card, but refused to slide it through the reader. "Just a hint?"

Mabel looked around. There was no one in line behind Summer. She closed her eyes and then opened them. "Let's just say… that Nancy changed her mind about letting you move in, but not about renting for at least six months."

Summer paid for the groceries in silence. That was a big hint. If they were only paying for one month, Luke must be paying for the other five. How could he do that? Could he afford to do that? Was it something he'd have done for anyone or was it because of his feelings for her?

Mabel must have had some idea of her thoughts because she said, "I guess you took my advice, huh? Cooking for a man always gets results."

"You on tomorrow, Mabel?"

"Yep."

"Okay, I'll see you then." Summer pushed her cart outside. She returned to her temporary home wishing she hadn't talked Mabel into spilling the beans. She didn't know if she should let Luke know that she knew or not and she couldn't tell anyone else to ask for advice. She thought he might be happier if she pretended not to know since he had wanted it that way. But Summer thought not telling would feel dishonest. She didn't think she had that good of a poker face either.

She hid in her room while her mom made dinner and was distracted while they ate. She spent the rest of the evening sitting in the window seat. At some point she remembered Emma's advice about her other problem. Relax. Maybe if she simply said thank you and let it go then Luke wouldn't feel funny about it.

Summer picked up her phone and held it. She closed her eyes. *God, help me be casual. And calm. I want to be casual and calm and not make this huge, huge thing sound like a big deal. Can we do that?* She opened her eyes and still felt overwhelmed. She wanted to pretend she didn't know, but knew that wouldn't work. She wasn't good with secrets. Luke would know something was up and that would be weird. She took a breath and touched his number.

94

Luke was a bit nervous when he saw who was calling. He was worried she was going to change their plans... that perhaps her guilt and gratitude were wearing off already. "Hi, Summer. What's going on?"

"Hey, Luke. I, um, had a question for you. Do you know what you want to have for dinner tomorrow?"

She was still coming. "Hadn't really thought about it yet."

"Well, I was thinking that I'll be at the Market for eight hours tomorrow so if we'll need any ingredients you don't have, then I'd rather pick those up before I leave than have to go back."

"That makes sense. How to you feel about breakfast for dinner?"

"I love it. I'm always too tired to have anything but cereal in the mornings. How do you feel about omelets?"

"Great. And I have eggs and cheese."

"What about some sort of veggie?"

"You mean we're going to be healthy?"

"Just a little bit. No mushrooms though, right? Broccoli?"

"I could live with that."

"Okay, um... there's something else."

Luke thought Summer's voice had changed slightly. He switched his phone to his other ear. "What else?"

"I sort of have a confession." He didn't say anything so she plowed on. "I found out what you did for us, how you changed Nancy Michealson's mind. Don't worry, my parents don't know and I won't tell them. I just... since I know I have to tell you how much I appreciate it. I can't believe you..." Summer clamped her mouth shut before she went from casual to gushing. "And that's it. Just thank you and I'll see you tomorrow."

Luke tossed his phone onto his couch. He wondered how Summer had found out, and so quickly. He knew the how didn't matter though. The only part that mattered was that she knew. That was not going to help the situation. He had been thinking about the way she appeared relieved when the siren interrupted on the swings and the way she had refused to face him on the couch. He was convinced that Summer was trying to make herself like him. She was happy to be with him when things stayed friendly, but faltered if he tried to make a romantic move. Her sense of obligation only went so far. But now... she didn't know that the rent wasn't a sacrifice for him. Was she going to make herself try harder?

Luke was still pondering that question when he arrived at his mom's for lunch on Saturday. She greeted him with a hug, which was somewhat unusual. "Hi, son," she said.

He followed her to the kitchen where something smelled delicious and chocolaty. The table in the next room was set for two with an embroidered tablecloth with white napkins and even the good china. "What's the occasion?" he asked.

"Saturday. It's my favorite day of the week, you know."

Luke tried to smile at her, but she didn't quite look at him. "Do you need any help?" he asked.

She shook her head and slipped her apron over her navy suit. "Just stand back."

He did as he was told. He knew better than to help when she didn't want it. Gloria pulled out a skillet and quickly put together a few grilled sandwiches with ham and Swiss cheese. While they were cooking, she pulled a pan of brownies out of the oven. Luke felt as though he was about to be buttered up for something. He hoped she didn't want any more furniture moved.

Lunch began very quietly. Both Fosters were preoccupied, though with different subjects. Gloria, however, feared that they were both brooding over Nikki. That horrible girl was back and Gloria didn't think she could warn Luke without admitting what had happened the last time. "Are you ready for a brownie?" she asked. "They have walnuts."

"Okay, let me get them." Luke returned to the kitchen and sliced two brownies. He put them on dessert plates and carried them to the dining room. He'd given himself a significantly larger piece because he'd been well trained.

"So it seems as though something is on your mind, Luke."

"Sort of."

"Is it a girl?" Gloria fished.

Luke sighed. There was no point in denying it. "Yeah, I've been seeing someone." His mother frowned at him, which was nothing like the reaction he expected. "I thought you'd be happy. Aren't you the same woman who's been trying to marry me off since I finished school?"

"Don't say it like that. I only want you to find someone who makes you happy. You don't... you don't look particularly happy at the moment."

"That's not her fault. She's wonderful. I'm just not sure it's going to work out."

96

Wonderful? Gloria snorted on the inside. What sort of mind games was Nikki playing? She said only, "Why not?"

"I'm not sure how to explain it." Luke didn't want to tell his mom why Summer might feel guilty because he wanted her to think only positive thoughts if they ever met. He also didn't want to explain her possible sense of obligation. He would never be able to convince her that helping the family had been his idea. She would assume Summer talked him into it.

"You don't have to tell me everything. Just generally what makes you think it won't work?"

"I guess I just think she's less interested than I am."

"Really?" That was certainly not the impression Nikki was going for.

"It isn't that shocking, Mom. You're just used to me."

"A woman who gets scared off by a harmless quirk isn't worth having."

Luke was finished with his brownie. He pushed the plate away. "Well, I haven't given up yet. We have a date tonight."

Gloria frowned again. "Are you sure she's not..."

"If you're worried about the money, I haven't told her."

"That doesn't mean she doesn't know."

"I'm pretty sure she doesn't."

"Luke," Gloria said as she braced herself, "she does know."

"How do you know that she knows? You don't even know who we're talking about."

"Nikki, right?"

"Nikki? Nikki Chapman?" Luke shook his head and Gloria immediately knew that she was the only one who had fallen victim to Nikki's mind games.

"Nikki told me you two were dating again and I saw you with her at church last week."

"She just showed up at church and that's the only time I've seen her."

"You're not dating Nikki?"

"No. Definitely not dating Nikki."

"In that case, I'll be happy to tell her off."

Luke was confused. "When did you talk to Nikki?"

"Sunday. She came by and..."

"She was here? Why would she come to see you?"

"She, um... wanted... she told me she was dating you again."

"Mom, what aren't you telling me?"

Gloria bit her lip nervously. Luke was going to be angry, but he'd forgive her. "I don't know how she found out. She knew about the money before she even asked you out the first time."

Luke sat staring at his mom, waiting for the rest of the story.

"She came to see me then, told me she intended to marry you unless I could convince her otherwise. You were... not interested in sharing details... I didn't know how much you did or didn't like her. But she was plain about her motivation and I... I paid her to stop seeing you."

"You did what?"

"It was... I regretted it right away. But I didn't want to take a chance on her taking advantage of you."

"So she came back now to try to get more money? How much did you give her?"

"Nothing. I hoped you were... you're older now so..."

"I mean the first time. How much did you pay her to stop seeing me?"

"It's not important."

Luke stood up and started pacing the room. "It's not important because I wasn't going to marry her. But what if I had wanted to?"

"Luke, sit down."

"No. What if I had wanted to marry her? What if I didn't care why she was with me?" He was thinking about Summer, thinking that he wanted to keep seeing her no matter what, realizing how much he had fallen for her already.

"Of course you'd care. You can't marry someone who doesn't love you."

"It was good enough for Dad." Luke was angry, but he still wished he could take back the words as soon as they left his mouth. His mom looked as though she'd been slapped.

She stood slowly and began to clear the lunch dishes.

"Mom, I'm sorry."

"He told you everything, huh?" She didn't look at him.

"I don't know. He told me some."

"He promised me he'd never tell you."

Luke didn't know what to say. He wished his dad was there to defend himself. He picked up a handful of dishes to take to the kitchen. His mom was standing by the sink. She was crying and it was his fault. She had also confessed to something he needed a little more time to process. He put his hand on her arm for a moment. "Look, Mom, I know you loved Dad and that you love me. Let's talk tomorrow when things are calmer."

"Don't leave yet," she said without turning around.

He squeezed her arm before he let go. "Bye, Mom."

Chapter 13

Summer almost braided her hair after her shower. She remembered the way her scalp tingled when Luke touched her hair though. She dried it a bit more and left it alone, hoping loose strands would be more tempting to his fingers. She put on a light green shirt with green plaid shorts and then sighed at the mirror. It was the third outfit she had put on. It looked good, but her purple bag would clash. The bag was something like a security object and she couldn't go without it when she was already nervous. And she really didn't have time to change again. She grabbed the bag without looking at the mirror and went downstairs.

She had heard Max and Leo shouting, "Take cover!" over and over from her room and wondered what they were up to. They were in the middle of the living room ripping a newspaper to bits and throwing handfuls of it into the air. Then they shouted and dove to the floor as they watched the paper flakes rain down. Summer found her mom in the kitchen opening and closing cabinets.

"I can't decide what to make," she said. "And it's not as though we even have that many choices." Megan put her hands on her hips as she faced her daughter. "But you don't care, do you, because you're not eating with us."

Summer smiled happily. "Do you know what the boys are doing?"

Megan looked at the ceiling for a moment. Summer recognized the silent prayer for patience before her mom nodded. "They know they have to clean it up before dinner. So while you're out tonight, I want you to find out whether next Friday or Saturday works better for Luke and make him come for dinner. We owe him."

Summer nodded obediently, glad that her mother had no idea how much they owed him. Then she went to the refrigerator to retrieve the veggies she'd stashed there after work. "See you later," she said as she made her way to the front door.

The butterflies she felt when Luke opened his front door were starting to feel familiar. He looked happy to see her and made those butterflies fight even harder for her attention. "Hi," she said.

"Come in... I see you brought something for us."

Summer crossed into the house and quickly tossed her bag into a corner. She held up the round plastic container. "Yeah, working at the Market does have occasional perks. They were making some kind of stir fry in the deli and I asked if I could have some omelet-worthy veggies. They're already diced."

"That's handy."

"That's why it's a perk."

"Should I put that in the fridge for a bit or do you want to get started right away?"

"I can wait."

"Okay, go sit." Luke tipped his head towards his living room and took the container into the kitchen. Summer went the direction he'd indicated. The space was very plain, but functional. She considered sitting in the middle of the couch so Luke would sit next to her. She brushed off the idea as way too obvious and claimed the end next to the recliner. He sat across from her as expected.

"How was lunch with your mom?" she asked.

"Pretty much awful actually."

"I'm sorry. What happened?"

Luke rubbed his forehead with the palm of his hand. "I found out about something that upset me, maybe more than it should have, and I made her cry."

"That *is* awful. Do you want to tell me about it?"

He did. He wanted to tell Summer everything she would hear. He wanted them to know each other well. "I have to start, um..." His eyes met hers with an apologetic glance. "Just stop me if you get confused, okay?"

Summer nodded and he leaned forward so that his elbows were on his knees. "Most of the awfulness was related to something about me that I don't think you know and I should tell you that first because of...the thing you do know."

Summer sucked her bottom lip between her teeth. She didn't want to tell him that she was already confused.

Luke said, "My family, we... we sort of have some money." He paused to see if she understood.

"You mean you're secretly a millionaire or something?"

Luke didn't laugh. He looked uncomfortable instead.

"Oh, wait... really!?"

"Yeah, I don't like to tell people, but... well, I didn't want you to think I drained my life savings to pay the rent."

"Honestly, I'm glad you told me. I was a little worried. Can I ask, um...I don't need to know, but..."

"Where did the money come from? My great-grandfather had some lucrative patents and then my grandfather invested well. My parents taught me not to squander it, which I hope I'm not doing by starting a risky company. It's likely that Game Smelters will never be profitable, but I think I'll be happy to say that I tried and I like to think I'm not wasting money by making jobs and... there really isn't room for the people though."

"You lost me on that last part."

"Oh, sorry... I skipped ahead. I was thinking that the company provides jobs *and* a yam float." He smiled slightly. "Mike's excited about the flying yams idea, but he doesn't know how to incorporate people."

"People on the float?" Summer asked.

"Mike wants to let his kids ride and apparently Zander has already told at least two of his friends that they can be on the float and I just think if you're going to have people on the float then they should somehow be part of it. But I guess I don't know what I'm talking about."

Summer gave a slight shrug. It didn't feel like a time to talk about Yam Fest. She wanted to go back to Luke sharing details of the argument with his mom. It was difficult to picture him getting upset with anyone. She knew everyone did occasionally, but he had kept his temper when she deserved otherwise and that made her curious about what was too much for him.

"Do you remember when I told you about Nikki?" he asked.

"Yes." Summer stretched out the word. Of course she remembered. She wondered if this was a new topic or an old one.

"What I found out today was why things ended so suddenly. Mom paid her to stop seeing me."

Summer's eyes widened. "She just really didn't like her?"

"I guess Nikki knew that... she knew about the money and was only pretending to like me to get her hands on some."

"In that case, I'm glad your mom got rid of her."

"Wait... you're on Mom's side?"

"Not exactly. Obviously, she should have told you about it, but I can see how that would have been hard for her. She didn't want to see you get hurt."

Luke didn't respond. He was still leaning forward and staring at the floor. He didn't see the floor though. He saw all the times his mom thought people were taking advantage of him. Just last week she had been concerned that his game changed direction somewhat. She hinted that his employees might not respect his authority, rather than accept that his team made a decision together.

He always thought she was irrational. The revelation about Nikki had stung because it proved there was a time his mom was right. Though he hadn't been falling for Nikki and might have ended the relationship himself soon, he hadn't had any idea of her scheme.

He was snapped from his thoughts by Summer's hand lightly touching his arm. "You okay?" The concern in her voice said she feared having said something he didn't like.

"Yeah, I... it's done and it was a few years ago anyway. I think I'm mostly feeling bad about how I reacted. I basically accused my mom of marrying my dad for *his* money."

"Oh, no."

"The thing is... that's not entirely untrue."

"She did marry him for the money?"

"He knew that though so it wasn't... it wasn't a trick or anything underhanded. I don't really know... Dad only told me his side."

Summer appeared interested and he wanted her take on it. "As a kid I only knew that they met where she worked. Dad was an accountant. Mom waited tables at the restaurant next door to his office. He met her there when he stopped in for lunch. That's pretty much all I cared to know. I didn't need any mushy details.

"But then Dad's last year or so we really talked a lot. He seemed to want to tell me everything he could about his life before he was gone. He told me that soon he started coming in for lunch most days and he'd come in later because the place would be fairly deserted and she'd have time to stick around and chat. Sometimes she'd even sit with him and they got to be pretty friendly over several months. Dad said he was completely nuts about her but didn't say anything because of the age difference.

"Then one day while they were talking, she just burst into tears. He already knew quite a bit about her family and that they were struggling financially. Mom was twenty-one. Three of her younger siblings were still in school and living at home. Her next sister, Ellie, had gotten married right out of high school. She figured the best thing she could do to help the family was give them one less mouth to feed. Mom's mom worked in a factory, but she had gotten laid off about two months before this and she was having some health problems. It had something to do with the veins in her legs. She had to have surgery, which got in the way of finding a new job *and* added medical bills. Mom was pretty much supporting her family with help from two of her younger brothers who had part-time jobs. The final straw, or the reason Mom broke down that day, was that Ellie had arrived at their house the night before with a suitcase. She admitted that her husband had been hitting her and that she needed to get out before the baby came. She was about seven months pregnant."

Luke paused in his story to take a breath. Summer waited for him to continue. She was hoping it would begin to sound happier and thought the fact that Luke seemed to be holding back a smile might be a hint. He said, "So I guess Dad's reaction to the sad story was to propose."

"Just like that?"

"Yep. He confessed that he was in love with her and that he had the means to support her whole family. He told her that if she would marry him then he would take care of everything."

"Apparently she said yes."

"Not right away. She told him that she wanted to think about it and give him an answer the next day. When she got home that night, her brother announced that he planned to drop out of high school to work full time. He was a senior and a very good student and she couldn't let him do that. She told her family that she was dating an accountant who might be able to help and she told Dad that she would marry him.

"Because of Dad's job and the fact that Mom was handling the family's finances, they were at first able to make it look as though he was just helping with paperwork and finding loopholes and stuff instead of slipping in extra cash. He even helped the three youngest siblings go to college. They were all really smart and got partial scholarships and need-based grants, too. He just kind of fudged the last bit to help them avoid debt. I don't think they know even now that he helped. Mom's mom, however, did eventually figure out what was going on. But by that time, Dad was part of the family so she accepted his help. Ellie even got

104

remarried a few years later to a very nice guy so things worked out pretty well for everyone."

"But what about your parents? They got married to solve a problem. That doesn't sound like... how did they make that work?"

"Keep in mind that I only know Dad's side of all this. I didn't want to hear about it, but he insisted on telling me in case I ever heard anything about it. He said there were rumors for a while about her marrying him for the money, which were probably because of his age and not because anyone knew anything. Dad wanted me to know that he never felt used because it was his idea. He told her that he didn't care that she didn't feel the same way about him. He was lonely and just wanted someone to come home to. She moved in when they got married but with separate bedrooms. Their plan was to stay friends. Dad said that got awkward really fast. He was married to a woman he loved who was sleeping in the next room and she *knew* how he felt. And that's when I made him stop talking."

Luke suddenly sat back in his chair and became much more animated. "I said, 'Dad, I don't care what kind of wisdom you are trying to impart. There is no way I'm going to sit here and listen to you tell me how Mom moved into your bedroom. You're going to say, "Eventually she fell in love with me, too. The end."' He laughed at that. I think he realized he was oversharing and he said, 'You're right, son. Eventually she fell in love with me, too. The end.'"

His reaction made Summer laugh as well. She was glad that Luke could look so happy talking about his dad even though he hadn't passed away very long ago. They must have been close. "That's a good story," Summer said. "But your mom didn't know that you knew all that?"

Luke shook his head. He stopped smiling as he remembered the earlier exchange with his mom. "Yeah, I'm not sure... They had almost thirty years together and even if there was a rocky start, most of it was very happy. I think maybe she feels as though she took advantage of him even though he didn't see it that way and that makes her ashamed or maybe she's worried I'll think less of her or maybe there's a part of the story Dad left out and that's what upset her." Luke sighed heavily. "I'm not sure what bothers her so much about me knowing and I hate the way it came out, but it might end up being better that she knows I know."

"Maybe. My mom said something like that when she told me about my dad or... well, why he didn't know about me. She said that sometimes when something is hard to talk about, it's just as hard to keep a secret."

105

"I hope so," Luke said. "I hope Mom feels a bit of relief and we can get back to normal right away."

"Did I tell you he died?"

"Your dad?"

"Yeah. He died in June but I just found out."

"How do you feel about that?"

"Honestly… I mostly feel bad that I don't feel bad."

"It doesn't upset you that you can't change your mind about meeting him?"

"Not really. It almost makes me relieved that it's no longer an option." Summer hoped that didn't make her sound too selfish. Luke didn't say anything and Summer wanted to move quickly past the awkward silence. "So are you hungry yet?" she asked.

He stood up. "I suppose we should get started."

Summer followed him into the kitchen where he pulled a skillet from a cupboard and put it on the stove. He got out a bowl and a whisk and opened the refrigerator. "You're starting to give the impression of someone who knows what he's doing."

Luke tried to narrow his eyes at her, but they were still smiling. "You doubted my cooking skills?"

"I did hear that you're a fan of the premade deli items."

He froze with a carton of eggs in one hand and the refrigerator door open in the other. "What else have you heard about me?"

"Only that Mabel thinks you're afraid of her."

"Don't tell her, but she does kind of scare me. Do you know that she actually wished me a happy birthday?"

"But that's nice."

"It would have been nice if I'd had any idea how she knew it was my birthday."

Summer laughed. "She does know things, but I've never heard her spread negative gossip. She wants to be friendly. And just for the record, when is your birthday?"

"May." Luke put a few more things on the counter. The mention of birthdays made him remember the necklace he'd made for Summer. It was still sitting in his truck and he still didn't know if he should give it to her. "For the record," he said, "I can cook a little bit. My mom made me help her a lot when I was in high school. She insisted it was a good skill to have. Now that I live alone and it might come in handy, it usually doesn't feel worth the effort."

106

"I don't blame you for that. Do you think it's terrible that I don't live alone?"

Luke quickly shook his head. "I wasn't in a hurry to move out either. In fact, after college I moved into a guest house on my parents' property. I had dinner with them nearly every night and wandered over there on a lot of weekends. If I had found a good office space in Port Harris, I'd probably still live there."

"I'm happy you came to Hartford."

"Me, too." He made himself look directly at Summer. She was definitely the biggest reason he was glad to be in Hartford. She did look happy he was there, too. Maybe it was wishful thinking, but she seemed to be willing him to come even closer. A voice in his head said that he could finally kiss her and he wanted to test that theory. He took a small step forward.

She turned quickly toward the counter and said, "How many eggs should I crack?"

All of them, he thought. She might as well drop all the eggs on the floor and forget about them for as much appetite as he had. He shook off the impulse to brood. He said, "I'd probably do three or four if it was just me. How hungry are you?"

She was suddenly not hungry at all. She tried to act naturally. "I guess I'll add six."

Luke nodded and opened the veggies she brought. It was an attempt to distract himself and it worked better than he expected. "Um, what exactly is this?"

"I didn't ask." Summer looked into the container he held out. "Looks like shaved carrots and some sort of shoots or sprouts. Those are onions. I don't know what those round things are." She gave him a rather sheepish look. "I trusted Shirley's judgment."

"Well, you know I frequent the deli and she hasn't let me down yet."

"If we smother them with enough cheese, it'll be good no matter what."

Luke smiled. "I'm not too worried about the veggies, but that is still an excellent idea."

Summer turned back to the eggs feeling a bit encouraged by his smile. Maybe she'd get a chance to make up for her blunder. She'd been thinking about kissing him all day in the hopes that she'd be ready. It only made her more anxious. She needed to relax and focus on having a good time. He'd try again and she wouldn't flinch.

The omelet was deliciously cheesy. They popped open a tube of cinnamon rolls for dessert and the scent lingered even while Summer helped with clean up. She could hardly breathe enough to enjoy it when Luke was standing so close to her by the sink. Her face warmed every time their arms bumped, which seemed to happen more than necessary. But he made no move.

They talked for a while afterwards and shared a few laughs. Summer was ready when he walked her to the door. She was still nervous, but happy nervous. He opened the door quickly when she expected him to stall.

Summer stopped before going outside. "Oh, Mom said I should make you come for dinner on Friday or Saturday. Those were her words. She didn't say invite she said make him come."

"Which day?"

"The one that works better for you."

Luke thought for a moment. "I guess Saturday." He kept his hand on the door, ready to close it behind her.

"Okay, um, bye then." She waved and walked down his sidewalk. She didn't look back when she heard the door close.

Luke leaned forward and let his forehead fall against the inside of the door. He didn't want that to be the end. He wanted to go after her, to give her the present he'd made, to beg her to stay longer. But no matter what he had tried to tell himself earlier, he did care why she was with him. He wasn't going to watch her try to make herself date someone she couldn't stand to kiss. It would be much easier on her if she didn't eventually have to reject him.

Chapter 14

Gloria watched Luke enter the church. Without looking around, he began walking towards their usual seats. He was wearing that same boring shirt and watching the carpet under his feet. She wished he would stop trying so hard to be invisible. She only had one hope for grandchildren. She immediately chastised herself for the thought. She appreciated the family she did have. It only mattered that she and Luke could get past the mistakes she had made.

"Hi, Mom," he whispered as he sat next to her. He lightly kissed her cheek before he grabbed a hymnal to look for the opening song. He hadn't kissed her in a long time and it nearly brought a tear of relief.

They went out to lunch afterward. Gloria turned down a few of her usual invitations for the time alone with Luke. Neither of them said more than small talk for a while after they were seated. Gloria decided to be the first to venture near the previous day's argument. "How was your date last night?"

"It was fun, but... I think it was the last one."

"Did she say something like that?"

"No, I'm just pretty sure she'd rather be friends and I'd rather not make her say that. You'd have liked her though. She told me she wanted to have lots of kids."

Gloria smiled. "That's not a bad thing, but I don't think I'd like anyone who isn't crazy about you."

Luke rolled his eyes only slightly before they landed on the plate that had recently been put in front of him. He pushed the noodles around with his fork for a minute. "I think Dad told me because he wanted to be sure I knew he was okay with it."

He sensed that his mom tensed up on her side of the table. He continued talking to his plate. "I'm sorry that I brought it up the way I did. I shouldn't have... I just want you to know that it doesn't bother me that you and Dad had an unusual start. I think it's more an interesting

109

story than anything to be embarrassed about. I hope you aren't." He lifted his eyes a bit.

"Do you forgive me for what I did with Nikki?"

He nodded.

"Are you sure?"

"Yes. We don't have to talk about her ever again."

"And you don't think I'm some sort of gold digger?"

"I really don't. I think it was complicated and that I can't judge either of you for something that happened years before I was born. And it sounds like you were in a pretty desperate place so if anyone took advantage…"

Gloria shook her head. "He didn't. We both knew it might be a mistake. We were blessed with a lot of happy years eventually. We even laughed together about some of the awkwardness in the beginning. But recently it's been harder to laugh at that. Your dad was gone only a few months before you moved to Hartford and the house is feeling so empty. I just think that if this is what your dad was feeling when he proposed then maybe… I don't know."

"I don't think so, Mom. He wasn't lonely in general. He was lonely for you. But you're not really unhappy, are you?"

"Just having a little trouble adjusting. But religious ed. classes will start soon and I'm looking at a few other ways to fill my time."

"Make sure you keep Saturday afternoons open."

"Of course," Gloria said. "That really is my favorite day of the week."

"This is terrible," Summer whined into her phone.

"What is?"

"Emma, I called Luke."

"It's about time. You can't complain every day about how much you want to talk to him without at least trying. What did he say that was terrible?"

"I got voicemail. I said I was just calling to say hi. Then I got a text from him about a half hour later, which was like two minutes ago. It says, 'Sorry I missed your call. Looking forward to Saturday.' He doesn't want to talk to me."

"You'll see him on Saturday and that's only two days away."

"He's only coming for my parents' sake. It's over and it's my fault."

"Just wait 'til Saturday and make sure he knows you're interested in him."

110

"How am I supposed to do that with my family there?"

Emma let out a slightly impatient laugh. "I'm not suggesting that you try to make out with him in front of your parents. I'm just saying, you know, smile a lot and look happy to see him. You can say a lot with your eyes."

Summer sighed sappily, thinking of the things Luke's eyes said. She didn't think hers could be nearly as forthcoming. "I guess I can try," she said.

"By the way, can I come?"

"On Saturday?"

"Yeah, I want to meet Luke. I think it'd be fun to tell him some of the things you've been saying about him."

"That's why you're not invited."

"Sounds like you could use my help."

"I'm already pathetic. I don't need to add another level by having someone else talk to him for me."

"You're not pathetic."

"Thank you, but I don't believe you."

"Do you believe that I need to go now?"

"All right. Talk to you later, Emma." Summer put her phone away and stared out her window. She wished she could have gotten Emma's opinion on the other part of her problem. She didn't want Luke to think that his money had anything to do with increasing her apparent interest. But he had said he didn't like telling people and that sounded like a good reason not to immediately blab it to Emma or anyone else. Summer's hope was that he told her only because he thought enough of her to know she wouldn't be swayed by it. She closed her eyes and thought of Luke coming to her house on Saturday. There was hope.

Saturday, however, did not live up to the hope. Luke did have dinner with Summer's family. He was polite and friendly to all of them. Max and Leo began to relax around him by the time Megan brought over some cookies. They thought it was hilarious when he stole Summer's cookie. She would have laughed if he'd looked at her at all. After dinner, the boys insisted he come upstairs to see the castle they had built out of LEGOs. Summer checked on them a few minutes later and saw that Luke was helping them add a few turrets.

He said he had to leave as he returned to the adults, that he had to meet Mike and Zander to work on the yam float while they still had some

111

daylight. That made sense as Yam Fest was only two weeks away. Summer still felt that he rushed out. Luke left with a friendly goodbye to the family as a whole. Summer went up to her room and tried not to cry.

She called Luke on Tuesday and got voicemail again. She called a few days after that and he answered the phone but only made small talk before making an excuse to hang up. She thought about trying to approach him at church, but his mom was there.

It was the Wednesday before Yam Fest when Summer found herself sitting at her temporary kitchen table watching Kyle. He had his usual stacks of papers and smiled slightly as Summer sat across from him. She watched him put one stack into the pocket of an accordion folder and shifted another stack into its place. He had one pen in his hand and another one tucked behind an ear. Summer sighed loudly and said, "I flinched."

Kyle looked up and forced his eyebrows together. "Excuse me?"

"Can I ask you about something?"

"Okay."

"It's about Luke."

Kyle squirmed visibly. "You want relationship advice?" He had noticed Summer moping around and that she hadn't seemed to have heard from Luke recently.

"I don't know who else to ask. Emma's no help."

Kyle put down his pen. "I'll try."

Summer looked over her shoulder. Her mom was upstairs helping Max and Leo get ready for bed so there was no one else around. "If I tell you something, will you promise not to tell anyone... including Mom?"

"Probably."

"Probably?"

"Well, you know there are some things I couldn't keep from your mom, but I don't think you'd ask me to keep a secret like that so... probably."

"Fine. The thing is... I..." Summer shifted in her seat and looked over her shoulder again. "I've never kissed anyone."

Kyle felt his ears get a bit warm. This was not going to be a fun conversation. Still, the news itself wasn't so bad. "Really?" he said. "I kind of thought Kevin..."

Summer shook her head.

"Tom?"

112

She let the hand that was under her chin fall to the table. "You do know what never means, don't you?"

"Right. Sorry. So why is this a problem?"

"Well…" She twisted a bit of hair around her fingers. "Luke tried and I… I flinched. I got scared and turned away and now he thinks it was because I didn't want him to and that's why he backed off."

"Okay."

"So what am I supposed to do?"

"You could become a nun."

Summer said, "Kyle," in a disapproving tone. It still made him smile because it was the same way the boys said, "Dad," when they were bothered by him.

"All right," he said. "You can't call him now?"

"I did. I called him a couple of times and he's obviously trying to politely avoid me. I think the message is that he's not interested in just being friends. I'm afraid if I try to ask him out again he'll think I mean a friendly thing and he'll say no. Then I can't… I mean, that would be it."

"And you can't just tell him?"

"Tell him what?" Summer said flatly.

"That you like him."

"Because I flinched. I think we've established that I'm a wimp at this. I need to convince him to see me so we'll have a little time for me to work up some courage or something."

Kyle cast his eyes over the stacks between them as though his lesson plan might somehow have a clue. Summer looked up at the sound of her mom coming down the stairs. She picked up a small set of crutches and turned around again as she said, "He wants these by the bed in case he gets up in the middle of the night."

Kyle and Summer nodded at her back. Max and Leo had not been deterred from jumping off the bunk beds before Leo sprained his ankle. He'd had the crutches for three days and Summer wondered if he'd figure out how to use them before his ankle healed. He seemed to prefer to hop.

"I think I actually have an idea," Kyle said suddenly.

"An idea for me?" she asked.

"Yeah. Leo won't be able to keep up with the Cub Scouts in the parade and we were trying to find someone who has a wagon we could borrow… but I think he'd be just as happy to ride with a float."

"You think I should ask Luke if Leo can ride in the truck with him?"

"And you. They make you line up very early so by the time you get to the end of the parade route, you'll have been stuck together for at least two hours. Surely that's enough time for you to tell him you want to see him again."

Summer felt her face break into a full smile. "That is a great idea," she said. Luke was way too nice to say no to a six-year-old with crutches. If she could see him one more time she'd be able to tell him how much she wanted to keep seeing him. Or at least tell him something.

Kyle smiled back. "Sometimes I surprise myself."

"Thanks. I'm going to call him now so you can go back to work." Summer ran up the stairs and heard Kyle begin to hum behind her. She poked her head into the boys' bedroom where her mom was reading a story.

"Hey, sorry to interrupt but I have a question for Leo." She focused on the boy in the lower bunk. "Since you can't walk in the parade, would you be okay with riding in a truck pulling a float?"

Leo threw his covers back as though the parade was about to start. "Can I?" he asked excitedly.

"I'm going to find out, but I wanted to be sure it was okay with you. Goodnight, Leo. Goodnight, Max."

As she walked away from the room, her mother called, "Thanks for getting him riled."

"You're welcome," Summer called back. She closed her bedroom door and picked up her phone. She considered calling Emma first, but pushed that idea away. The more time she spent thinking about it, the more likely she was to think of a reason it wouldn't work, or otherwise talk herself out of it. She closed her eyes as soon as she heard ringing. *God, help me. Just help me.*

Luke had expected Summer to feel relieved when he backed off. He had expected her not to call and didn't know how to handle the surprise, yet again, of seeing her name on his phone. He wanted to talk to her but didn't trust himself not to ask her out. He didn't want to snub her either. It wasn't her fault that he wanted more than she could offer.

"Hi, Summer."

"Luke, um, how's the float coming?"

"Well, Mike is sure it will be ready in time."

"You're not?"

"I would be if he'd stop changing his mind about things."

"Okay, so I actually called to ask you a favor about the float."

114

"No, you can't borrow it afterwards."

Summer's laugh came through the phone as if she was right next to him. He sat on his couch and closed his eyes, trying to imagine she was there. She said, "That's not it. Leo had a slight mishap the other day and sprained his ankle."

"Oh, no. What happened?"

"He and Max were jumping off the bunk beds."

"Ouch. Is he stuck on crutches?"

"Yeah, that's where the favor comes in. He was going to walk with the Cub Scouts in the parade, but he won't be able to keep up now. I wondered if you might be willing to let him ride in your truck so he can still be in the parade. I'd come, too. We're not asking you to babysit. Not exactly anyway." She paused and held the phone tightly in anticipation.

"Okay. We're supposed to line up by 10 am. I'd have to pick you up a little before that and it sounds like there will be a lot of waiting around. Are you both up for that?"

"Yes. I'll bring something for Leo to read or play with just in case though."

"That sounds like a plan."

"I really appreciate you doing this, Luke."

He winced before he said, "You're welcome." He wished Summer could feel something for him other than gratitude. More gratitude was probably not going to help.

"So, um, did you get things patched up with your mom?"

"Yeah, as much as ever. She still thinks I'm going to disappear the moment lunch is over if she doesn't have some sort of job for me. This last Saturday she had me change a couple of light bulbs. Then just when I thought I was getting off easy, she announced that she had to clean under the rug."

"Under the rug?"

"There's this huge rug in the living room and she wanted to clean underneath it so I had to move the furniture off it and roll it up so she could clean. Then we waited around until the floor dried so I could unroll the rug and put the furniture back."

"That's sound like fun," Summer said dryly.

"Fun is not the word I would use. But we talk while we work, or while I work, and it makes her happy. I do have limits though. If she

115

ever hands me a paintbrush I'm going to say, 'Mom, let's play Scrabble instead.'"

Summer laughed again and said, "You don't paint?"

"Not anymore."

"Sounds like there's a story there."

"We're having lunch on Sunday."

"You and your mom?"

"Yeah, sometimes we only see each other at church, but we planned ahead for lunch because I won't see her Saturday."

"Oh, right. You'll be done with the parade before noon though. You can't just do lunch a little late?"

"We need to dismantle the float right away. I'm putting some of the stuff in storage and then I need to return the trailer."

"Why don't you paint anymore?"

Luke made a sound that was something like an amused sigh. "My mom made me paint one of the bedrooms when I was in high school. She left me supplies while she was off at some volunteer thing. I spent what felt like the entire day painting the room. She came back and looked at it and said, 'Maybe this isn't the right color after all.' I said, 'Mom, it's wonderful because I already finished.' She shook her head and said, 'No, this isn't going to work.' A few days later she gives me supplies and says she found the right color. I open up the can and it's like exactly the same thing that's already on the walls. So I asked her if there was some sort of mistake. She said something like the first one was blue ice cubes and the second was blue icicles. They were both barely blue-tinted white. She insisted it'd look different on the wall, but it didn't. I wanted to paint only one wall and see if she'd notice. She was home that day though and kept checking on me. She actually helped for a bit, too. But I still say it was the same color. I'm not doing that again."

"Does that only apply to your mom then? What if I asked you to paint something for me?"

Summer was only kidding around. It reminded Luke that he needed to get off the phone before he started thinking about some sort of future together… one in which Summer might ask him to paint a room. "I guess I did a little painting on the float so it's not completely out of the question. I should go now before you trick me into telling you what the float looks like."

"Oh, okay. Bye." Summer hung up with mixed emotions. On the one hand, Luke had agreed to spend time with her on Saturday and that

116

had been her goal in calling. On the other hand, he had to know that Mabel already told her about the float so his reason for getting off the phone was an obvious excuse not to talk any longer. That didn't sound like someone who was excited about the plan for Saturday.

That plan changed slightly when Luke considered his very limited experience driving a truck with a trailer behind it. He preferred to make as few turns as possible, which made it much easier to pick up Summer and Leo before the trailer was attached. Fortunately, Summer said it would be no problem for them to be ready earlier.

That appeared to be true because she opened the door before he knocked. "Hi," she said with a smile. "Leo's been watching for you." Sometimes it was nice to have a little brother to take the blame. Leo had been looking out the window, but he hadn't been the only one. Summer had watched Luke jump out of the now familiar red truck and stuff his keys in his pocket in a move that also felt familiar.

When she opened the door, she noticed that his hair was still damp. She blushed as thoughts of how his hair got wet popped into her head uninvited. "It seems like it's been a long time since I've seen you," she said.

Luke nodded slightly. He was thinking the same thing. He wanted to put his arms around her. That would not have been appropriate even if Kyle wasn't sitting at a nearby table putting a puzzle together with Max. "Hi, Kyle. Hi, Max."

"Good to see you again, Luke. Thanks for making room for these two." Kyle gestured to Summer and to Leo who was right behind her with two crutches and one big grin.

"I'll be happy to have company," Luke said before he turned to Summer. "You ready?"

She nodded and looked at Leo. "Say goodbye to Max and your dad."

"Why do you always say *your* dad instead of just dad? Isn't he your dad, too?"

Kyle cleared his throat as though he was going to answer for her, but he wasn't fast enough. Summer said, "I say your dad because he is your dad. But you're right, he's mine, too."

She didn't look at Kyle, but she knew he understood because his voice sounded slightly unnatural when he said, "Have a good time, guys."

Leo waved in the general direction of his dad and brother before he stuck his crutches under his arms. He managed to use them through the doorway. When he reached the porch steps though, he handed the crutches to Summer and hopped down the steps. He had hopped all the way to the passenger door of Luke's truck before she could give them back.

"Are you sure he couldn't keep up with the Cub Scouts?" Luke asked.

"It's a long parade. Hang on a second." Summer went to Kyle's car nearby and grabbed a booster seat from it. She put it in the truck before helping Leo climb in.

"This is so cool," Leo said. "I never get to sit in the front."

Chapter 15

Mike's brother had a barn just outside of town where the Game Smelters team had been working on the float. Leo spent the short drive there asking what all the knobs and gauges on the dash were for. Luke was very patient, even joking about what some of the symbols meant. Mike was waiting to help get the trailer hitched and the barn closed up. Then he left to pick up his kids and get into costume. On the way back into town, Luke asked Summer what she thought of the float.

"I'm impressed. I can't believe you all put that together in only three weeks."

"Are you just being nice?"

"No, really... it's good."

"It's not too..."

"I don't know what you're going to say, but no. You haven't seen the other floats yet. Compared to some I've seen, 'First Yam on the Moon' is downright inspired."

A large banner on each side showed the title of the float. In the middle was a moon-like sphere. A large yam was on top of it planting a Game Smelters flag. Mike and the other riders would be wearing astronaut suits. There were dark blue streamers around the edges with silver stars.

They looked at some of the other floats as they got into position. One was called "Green Eggs and Yam." Summer rolled her eyes at it. "Someone does Green Eggs and Yam like every other year."

The float for Fred's had a Yam Circus theme. Various yams were positioned as though they were performing circus acts, including a tightrope walker and a lion tamer. Summer said, "The acts are different, but that's the same theme as last year and it was better when Jimmy was juggling yams. They won actually."

"Who's Jimmy?"

"Someone I graduated with. He works for the police department so I think he's stuck doing crowd control this year."

There was another float with a huge pile of yams in the middle and a sign with the words "Yam Mountain." Summer bit her lip as she studied it. "I don't think I get that one."

"I'm not the yam float expert you are," Luke said, "but I don't think there's anything to get. I think someone was out of ideas."

"Can we climb the yam mountain?" Leo asked.

Summer shook her head. "We have to stay in the truck."

"There's a hill behind my parents' house that I liked to climb when I was a kid," Luke said.

Leo's face lit up. "Is it still there?"

"Yes."

"Can you take me sometime?"

"I don't know, Leo. You definitely can't climb any hills until you get that boot off your foot."

"How about after?"

"We'd need to see what your parents said."

"If they said it was okay?"

Summer could see that Luke was regretting bringing up the hill. She knew she was the reason. Luke couldn't come out and say that it might be weird to spend time with Leo if he wasn't dating Leo's sister. Luke expected the parade to be the last time they saw each other. Summer wanted to work on that. "Maybe we can talk Luke into taking both of us to see this hill, but let's wait until the doctor gives you permission before we worry about making plans. Are you ready for the parade?"

Leo nodded.

Luke looked at his watch. "We still have about fifteen minutes until it starts and we're number forty so it'll be a little bit."

"Okay, let me see what I brought." Summer picked up her purple bag from the floor and unzipped it. Her hair fell forward when she leaned over and it stayed like a curtain covering her search through the bag. Luke fought the urge to reach across Leo to push the hair back.

Leo suddenly tugged on his sister's arm. "Can we trade seats?" he asked. "I want to sit by the window so I can wave."

Summer moved her hair behind her ear as she turned to face the two guys in the truck. Leo had a hopeful look on his face and was still tugging her arm. Luke seemed to be focused on the back of Leo's head. She couldn't tell what he thought of the suggestion. "Yeah, I guess so," she said, thinking that would make at least two people happy.

The switch would have been a lot easier without the booster, but Summer managed to make it happen. She got Leo buckled again and then reached for her own seatbelt.

Summer was not the first person to accuse Luke of being too nice for his own good. Watching her strap herself into the seat right next to him was the first time he thought any of those people might be right. Her hair smelled like coconuts and the entire right side of his body sensed her nearness. He was torturing himself to be nice to the little brother of someone who balked at the idea of anything more than friendship. It was going to be a long parade.

Summer turned and flashed Luke a smile when she was settled and had passed Leo some sort of electronic toy. "He won't even notice when we start moving now."

Luke put his hands on the steering wheel because he didn't know what else to do with them. "Would you believe this is the first time I've ever been in a parade?"

"Of course I believe you," she said. "But I am surprised."

"I think I passed up a few opportunities. It just was never something I wanted to do."

"I get that about you."

"You get what?"

"You're not an attention seeker."

"Is that bad?"

Summer shook her head. As far as she was concerned, it was fabulous. She didn't think he'd still be single if he'd been trying to get anyone's attention.

Luke gestured out the front window. "Here comes Zander."

Three boys in their early teens approached the driver's side. Luke rolled the window down the rest of the way. "Hey, guys," he said. "You all ready?"

"We've been checking out the competition," Zander said. "We definitely have a chance."

One of his friends snorted. "I still cannot believe how lame the hair place's float is."

"Is that Yam Mountain?" Luke asked.

"No."

"Wait, let me." Zander gently shoved his friend out of the way and held up his hands as he began to explain. "There's two yams in the middle of it and they're each holding a tin can and there's a string between them. Then there's a third yam with a light bulb on top of it and underneath him it says Alexander Yam Bell."

They shared a short laugh before one of the boys pointed out Mike approaching.

"I guess you better climb aboard," Luke said.

They all thanked him for letting them be part of it and Mike stopped by the window to say hello as well. When he ushered his kids towards the float, Luke looked over his shoulder as he opened the rear window. He caught a strange expression on Summer's face. "You don't mind if we keep that open?" he asked. "I want to be able to hear the yelling if anyone falls off the back."

Summer recovered from her hopes and disappointment. For a moment, she had thought Luke was about to put his arm around her. She said, "You are planning to drive slowly, right?"

"Of course." He lowered his voice and added, "But the other day, one of Zander's friends fell off the thing when it was holding still."

Summer laughed. "Probably a good call on the window then."

A woman in a red shirt appeared as if from nowhere at Luke's window. "Parade's starting," she said in a bossy voice. "Watch for your entry signal." She moved on without waiting for a response.

Summer nudged Leo. "We're getting ready. Probably about time to put that away."

He looked around for a moment. "Oh, they're moving," he said. "Look over there. It's the parade."

"Yes, it is," Summer said. She leaned towards the floor on Leo's side to put his toy in her bag. When she sat up again, she flipped her hair back and caught Luke across the face. He jumped slightly. "Oh, no." She turned to him with an apologetic expression. "I just got you with my hair, didn't I?"

"It's okay. It didn't hurt, just surprised me."

"I'm really sorry."

"It's really okay. He made so little sense."

Summer held her mouth closed, but she was fighting a losing battle. Luke could see that she was trying not to laugh. He turned towards the front and exhaled slowly. "I thought you were okay with me being weird."

122

"I am. I'm not laughing *at* you. It's just that you lost me right when you said someone else didn't make sense. That was funny." She bumped his arm with her elbow. "Now tell me who else didn't make sense."

"One of Zander's friends." Luke tilted his head back towards the trailer for a moment and otherwise kept facing forward. "They're both named Ryan. Anyway, we were putting the moon on the float and he accidentally hit Zander with it, almost knocked him over, and he was trying to explain that it would have hurt more if we were on the actual moon. He said the moon weighs less here like people weigh less on the moon or something like that. He had us all laughing so hard I think that was my favorite day of working on the float."

"So you're definitely doing it again next year, right?" Summer teased.

"That would be funnier if Mike and Zander weren't already brainstorming for the float they think we're doing." He glanced in Summer's general direction with an amused expression.

Summer was thinking of Emma's advice to tell Luke with her eyes how she felt. She didn't think she'd be able to do that even if he wasn't refusing to make eye contact. Her mouth wasn't ready to say it either. But she couldn't finish the parade without him knowing he was wrong about her not being interested. A surge of adrenaline hit her with a new idea. His hands were resting on the bottom of the steering wheel. She pictured running her fingers along the back of his hand until he opened it enough to accept hers. That would be a pretty clear message and she thought she had enough courage to send it.

Just as she was ready to try, Luke moved his hands to restart the truck. "Looks like we're next," he said. "Are your waving hands ready, Leo?"

The 6-year-old beamed as he held both his hands up. His general shyness apparently did not apply to parades. He began waving as soon as there were people waving back. Luke and Summer figured that there was enough waving going on around them that they could simply relax and enjoy the ride, at least as much as either of them was able to relax.

A few blocks in Luke said, "Are those people taking notes?"

Summer looked where he was looking. "I think so. Most people just use their phones to take pictures of the floats they might want to vote for, but some people take notes."

"I wonder what people might be writing about ours."

"That it's awesome of course."

Luke smiled. "What do you think people really think? Not about the float exactly, but about me being new. Is it cool that I jumped right in with a float or am I an outsider trying to fit where I don't belong?"

"That's an interesting question," Summer said. "I'm sure it helps that Mike was the brains. And that everyone knows he was. I think people have mostly been pretty welcoming of new entries. I'm not sure, but you might be ruffling a few feathers with Zander and his friends though."

"How so?"

"They don't work for Game Smelters."

"I didn't know there was anything in the rules about that."

"Oh, there isn't. Officially, anyone who sponsors a float can ask anyone he wants to participate. But there are some people who think it should be limited to the employees or members. I know a few people gave Jimmy a hard time for riding on Fred's float last year."

"Sour grapes perhaps?"

Summer nodded. "That's definitely a factor. I notice people tend to get more bent out of shape if it looks like someone was recruited for a specific talent rather than a relationship to the sponsor."

"I'm not sure I fully appreciated what I was getting into when I signed up for this."

Summer waved just then and said to Leo, "Grandma and Grandpa are on this side."

Leo waved across Summer and Luke and then returned to sticking his arm out the window on his side. Summer realized that the parade was the fast part. They were almost halfway done with it already. She decided it was time to try an idea she'd planned out while still anticipating the event.

"Luke," she said, "are you going to tell me what you all have planned for the bonfire if you win?"

He shook his head. "I couldn't even if I wanted to because I don't know."

"You didn't plan anything?"

"I told Mike that he'd have to light it without me so he told me that if I wasn't going to participate then I didn't get to know. He and Zander do have something cooked up."

"Are you going to the bonfire?"

"I don't know. I guess I have to go if we win to support my team, but I'm not counting on that. I am a little curious what all the fuss is about so… maybe."

"You should go. It's my favorite part of Yam Fest."

"Mine, too," Leo added, though at the moment it was hard to believe the parade wasn't his favorite part. He was still waving wildly.

"I guess I'll probably go," Luke said.

Summer tried to push back some nerves as she twisted some hair around her finger. "A lot of people bring dates to the bonfire."

Luke didn't immediately respond. He didn't know if it was a simple observation or a hint. Was Summer suggesting he ask her? Was she still trying to make herself like him because she felt like she owed him? Had she not yet figured out that was what she was doing? It would be insulting to both of them if he pointed out the way she recoiled when he'd tried to kiss her. Luke tried to tread lightly. "A date to a bonfire? Is that... well, I don't know what it's like, but it doesn't sound like a romantic thing."

"It can be," Summer said. "It's dark and the fire makes wonderful crackling noises. You have to find a good spot though. Not too close to a crowd or someone who's had too much to drink. If you can find a good place, usually on the far end of the field, you can watch the fire from a distance and there are some delicious smells and the sounds of music or laughter from the stage. Sometimes the fireflies will be out and it's..." Summer pressed her lips together suddenly, thinking she might have gotten a bit carried away.

Luke had seen the dreamy look on her face and it was the end of treading lightly. "Will you let me take you?"

"Yes," Summer said quickly. She didn't have to think about it and she didn't want him to sense any hesitation. "The high school is only three blocks from where we're staying so it's probably easiest if you come over and we walk from there." The bonfire was held in a field next to the high school so its lot was used for parking.

"Okay. It starts at seven, right?"

"People start gathering at seven, but it'll be nearly eight before they light the fire. We could plan on leaving my house a little after seven."

Luke nodded. It looked as though he was going to say something else, but was interrupted by a loud horn. There had been occasional honks since the parade started. This was from the car right behind them and was loud enough that they felt it. It got Leo's attention.

"Hey, can *we* honk the horn?" he asked.

"It's right here. Can you reach it from over there?"

Leo reached out and blared the horn for a full five seconds before Summer picked his hand up and said, "That's probably enough."

125

"Can I do it again?" he asked. He was looking at Luke, probably because he thought Luke was more likely to say yes than because it was Luke's truck.

"Okay," Luke said, "but just quick taps. Don't hold it down."

Leo reached over again and pressed out some shorter sounds. It was difficult for him to reach and every time Leo honked the horn, he knocked Summer into Luke. She eventually leaned into him as though she was avoiding being knocked and almost wished Leo had asked about the horn sooner.

Chapter 16

"I can't believe I missed you," Summer said into her phone.

"I can," Emma answered. "You looked so cozy with Luke, I'm surprised you noticed anyone was watching the parade."

"Cozy? Just because we happened to be sitting next to each other…"

"Whose idea was that anyway?"

"It was Leo's actually. He wanted me in the middle so he could wave out the window."

Emma laughed. "I bet he had to work real hard to convince you."

"All right. I admit I liked the idea."

"I know you did. And I do hope things go well for you tonight."

"I'm still sad that you're going to miss the bonfire."

"People in the city just aren't very sympathetic," Emma said with a sigh. She worked at a restaurant in Port Harris and couldn't get the night off. When she tried to switch with a coworker, he laughed at her reason. Then he said no.

"You'll have to come over tomorrow so I can tell you all about it."

"Of course. As long as you don't just mean the fire. I should get ready though. I'm supposed to be there at two."

Summer put her phone away and went back to her closet. After church she had the typical pancake brunch with her family and then she decided to get something accomplished. All the clothes they hadn't immediately grabbed from the house had been sent off to be cleaned. The boxes of freshly laundered clothes had arrived almost a week ago and Summer's were still sitting unopened in her bedroom. The rest of the family's boxes were mostly unopened as well. Since they were going to pack up and move home soon it didn't feel worth the effort to put things away. Summer intended to leave most of the items in the boxes, but there was a particular yellow top she wanted to wear to the bonfire. She was only putting a few things away to give her room to search.

What she was trying to accomplish was a little time by herself. She was excited and didn't need either of her parents to see the goofy smile that came over her when she thought of seeing Luke that night. She was also scared. She'd been screwing things up with him from the beginning and even more than the parade, this night felt like her last chance to show him they would be good together.

Summer spent most of the afternoon trying to read or otherwise convince herself she was not watching the time. It still passed quickly and she was back at the table for dinner with her family. They were going to head to the field as soon as they finished eating. Max and Leo thought it would be fun to watch the volunteers set up. The boys wouldn't be allowed to stay very late so their parents were okay with going early.

Summer said goodbye to her family and then found a place at the front of the house to camp out by a window. As Luke arrived, she realized that it wasn't the truck that seemed an odd choice for him but its color. He was wearing the same thing he'd had on for church, tan pants and a plain white polo. Summer was fairly sure that was the flashiest she'd ever seen him. It didn't make him seem boring at all, just steady and constant. He'd nearly reached the door when he swiped his hand across his forehead. It was becoming a familiar gesture that was more likely due to nerves than hair.

Luke knew that taking Summer to the bonfire was a bad idea. He wanted to see her again. There was no doubt about that. But even though she had used the word date, he felt sure that her heart wasn't in it. He knocked lightly on the door and Summer answered quickly. She already had her bag over her shoulder and she came out and locked the door behind her. Then she said, "Hi."

"Hi. You look great."

"Thanks." Digging through the boxes earlier had not been a waste of time.

"You always look so colorful."

"Colorful?"

"I mean that as a good thing. You look, I don't know, bright and happy."

She smiled to herself. She looked bright and happy because he was there. "I tried to say hello at church this morning. You didn't see me."

"No, I didn't."

"I know. That wasn't a question. If I wasn't sure I'd be accusing you of ignoring me."

128

He looked mildly amused but there was something in his expression that she couldn't read and that made Summer nervous. His eyes typically telegraphed his emotions so clearly this felt as though he was deliberately masking something. She stuffed her hands into her pockets to try to nonchalantly wipe off her sweaty palms.

Luke thought again how much of a mistake this night was. She appeared to be guarding against an attempt to hold her hand and he wasn't even going to try. He resolved to do his best to keep things friendly and not make her uncomfortable. Then he could go home and try again to get over her.

"Well," he said, "I only know that I didn't get a call last night. Have you heard who the winning float was?"

"Yeah, Emma called me after she looked at the list."

"There's a list?"

"The Chamber of Commerce posts the top ten. Game Smelters was number eight. Congratulations."

"I guess that's good news. Who was number one?"

"The Band Boosters."

"What did their float look like?"

Summer stopped walking long enough to turn and watch Luke's reaction. "It was Yam Mountain."

"What!? How in the world did Yam Mountain win?"

"You're gonna have to learn that sometimes it's not just about the float. Small town politics can be tricky. Sometimes people will vote for an organization they think got the shaft the previous year or for some reason that doesn't have anything to do with the parade. There was this one year – I was only nine or ten so the details were over my head – but apparently the mayor and the town council were having some sort of dispute. I think it had to do with signs downtown. I guess there were enough people on the mayor's side that they successfully wrote her in as the winner even though she didn't even have a float. She was just riding in a car with a yam corsage. And of course she wasn't expecting to win so she didn't have anything planned for the bonfire.

"She wrote up a proclamation that named Saint Mary's as the honorary winner to light the fire in her place. Saint Mary's is a school for kids with special needs. They're outside city limits and not eligible for the contest, but they have a float every year anyway that's just the kids holding yams they decorated. Of course there were people who said the mayor did that to earn points because she was about to face an election. But I

129

think her popularity was already established by the write-in campaign for her non-existent float. And anyway, the Saint Mary's kids and teachers had this really long log – I think it might have been a telephone pole – and they put a torch on the end and just ran all the way across the field with it like a battering ram. It was actually pretty cool."

"So is the marching band in a feud with someone or are there just a lot of kids in the band?"

Summer smiled. "There's no feud that I know of. The number of kids might have helped, but I think mostly they won because word got out that if the Band Boosters won then a couple of majorettes were going to light the fire with flaming batons. I'm guessing people wanted to see that."

"I think I would like to see that."

"It's a good thing I talked you into coming then."

"I might have come on my own," Luke said, "but I'll be happy to have you explain things to me. Mike said something about making sure I stop at the information table, but it felt like he was setting me up for something."

Summer laughed. "He probably meant the library. They have a yam information table set up every year with facts about yams versus sweet potatoes. But the woman who mans it, she's on some kind of mission to have this whole weekend renamed the Sweet Potato Festival. She will rail to anyone who will listen about all the inaccuracies going on. She talks about how all the floats actually have sweet potatoes and about the Methodist church's bake sale that sells sweet potato pies labeled, wrongly, yam pies. I once heard her say that she doubted more than a handful of people in all of Hartford had ever laid eyes on an actual yam."

"I'm not saying it matters, but why isn't it a sweet potato festival?"

"I really don't know," Summer said. "But it's been Yam Fest for something like fifty years and I think we all know they're actually sweet potatoes. I looked up the difference once and it was almost sort of interesting. I still don't care if I'm calling a sweet potato a yam. It's a Hartford tradition."

Luke agreed with her assessment. It wasn't as though a yam or a sweet potato was going to land on the moon any time soon.

Summer asked, "Did your mom try to get you to do any painting today?"

"Oh, she tried to convince me it was bed day already. I told her I didn't have the time for that and she settled for having me dust pretty much everything in the house that requires a stepladder."

"What's bed day?"

Luke launched into an explanation of his mom's need to have crisply unused guest rooms at all times. By the time he was finished, they had arrived at the edge of the field. "Wow," he said, "this is more than I... Mike told me there was a stage and a fire and I... I guess I pictured both of those smaller with not much else going on. This is quite an event."

They were approaching several sets of bleachers around a stage and not-yet-lit bonfire next to a large pile of wood. There was a fire truck and an ambulance standing by and beyond the main area were several odd tables or stations of activity. It was still somewhat early and already hundreds of people were milling about.

Summer checked her watch. "I'll give you a quick tour of the area and then we'll try to find a spot to watch them start the fire."

"Okay. Can you start by explaining the cauldron?"

"I'll try." There was amusement in her voice. "Those are guys from the American Legion. They're making yam butter. The thing is though, no one really knows what yam butter is. They pick someone each year – and don't ask me how that's decided because I don't know – to make the recipe. It starts the same every year with them boiling the yams in the giant pan that does sort of look like a cauldron. There's a spigot in the bottom where they drain out the water. Then a few guys will surround it with giant wooden spoons to mash them up. Then whoever made the recipe will either make a big show of adding crazy ingredients or try to add everything in secret. There doesn't seem to be a middle ground. And when it's all ready they put it in jars to sell it as a fundraiser. A lot of people, including my parents, will buy some because it's a good cause and/or out of curiosity. I'm usually afraid to try it. Once it was so spicy that Kyle threw out the jar after one taste."

Luke was enjoying Summer's details. He'd have let her talk even if it wasn't his first Yam Fest. She explained the bake sales and which one had the best goodies. She introduced him to a few people she knew and explained how she knew them after they left. She pointed out the information table they were going to avoid. She was teasingly showing him where he could sign up for an open mic slot when someone called Luke's name. He turned to see two of his old interns approaching. Joey had called out and Lauren was with him.

"Hey! This is a surprise," Luke said. "What are you two doing here?"

Joey was dressed typically with a tie of black and silver. He said, "It was Lauren's idea. We were both home for the weekend and she asked me if I wanted to come check this out. I haven't decided if it was a good idea yet."

"Neither have I," Lauren said. She was looking at Summer so Luke made some introductions. He didn't notice how she was looking at Summer.

Joey was looking at the large pile of wood. "What time do they light the fire?"

"Should be soon," Summer said. "We were just going to see if there are any seats left."

"Do you want to look with us?" Luke asked.

"It's pretty crowded. I doubt there's room for all of us." Lauren turned away quickly. "C'mon, Joey."

Joey shrugged uncertainly as he began to follow her. "Glad we ran into you," he said. "Have fun."

Luke was puzzled as to why Lauren seemed upset. He guessed that she simply wasn't excited about turning the night into a double date. He didn't blame her. Even though it wasn't good for him, he preferred to be alone with Summer. They weren't exactly alone though. They squeezed into two seats at the end of the third row from the top.

Among those going up and down the stairs in search of open places, Luke recognized the woman from "Things to Do." She recognized him as well. "Oh, hi," she said. "How did that little project work out?"

"Fine."

Jill looked at Summer for a moment and Luke was afraid she was about to ask her how she liked the necklace he hadn't given her. Instead, she turned back to Luke and said, "I get it. Work in progress." Then she winked and continued her search for a seat.

Luke said, "I bought something from her store recently," to explain the brief exchange.

He was vague on purpose and Summer noticed. It felt as though he was averting questions rather than answering them and she was already unsettled by the run-in with the former interns. She had started the evening thinking that all she had to do was be encouraging. Her doubts were growing about there being anything to encourage. He'd been keeping a friendly distance and invited others to join them. She was beginning to wonder if she had been wrong about why he backed off before.

Then a very tall man with very little hair stepped onto the stage and tapped the microphone.

"Who's that?" Luke asked.

Summer shrugged. "I *think* that's the mayor."

"Hey, I actually found something about Hartford that you don't know."

Luke was only teasing, but Summer's growing insecurity made it feel like a jab about the fact that she'd hardly stopped talking since they arrived. Was she boring him that much?

The mayor – Summer was right – spoke only for a minute. He thanked everyone for coming and thanked all the parade participants especially. He reminded everyone to try to clean up after themselves and then announced the winning float. As he left the stage, about a dozen high school kids with drums marched onto the field. Two majorettes took positions on each side of the fire and began twirling. Soon, two girls in front lit their batons and grabbed a second so that it appeared each was holding two circles of fire overhead. The drumming paused and the crowd watched as both girls kept one baton spinning off to the side and stuck the other into the base of the waiting fire. They doused their batons as the fire started and the drumming began again. The air filled with cheers and applause as all the kids marched off the field.

All around them, people began to stand and stretch and generally flee the stands. "Where is everyone going?" Luke asked.

"The first few slots on stage are reserved for kids. Most people think that's a good time to check out the tables. The bleachers will fill up again if it sounds like someone good is on stage."

"Do you want to walk around, too, or would you rather sit for a while?"

Summer glanced at the stage. A girl who looked about Leo's age was pulling a violin out of a case. "I guess we can walk," she said. She wanted to go someplace quiet where they could talk about what was going on between them. She had no idea what to say, but hoped maybe Luke would say something.

He stood up and offered his hand as she climbed out of her seat. He let go too soon for her to feel as though it cleared anything up. At the bottom of the stairs, he looked to her for direction. The girl on stage was slowly scratching out the notes to Mary Had a Little Lamb. Summer gestured away from the stage.

They walked quietly past a crowded bake sale and a booth with a pond of rubber ducks. Summer stopped in an open area where they were more or less alone and turned back to face the fire. Sparks were dancing above it and they were close enough to the American Legion guys that whatever they were cooking up smelled like pumpkin pie fresh from the oven. It was a beautiful night that Summer wasn't enjoying.

She inhaled deeply. "When you told me there was a love triangle in your office... you didn't say you were part of it."

"I don't know how I talked him into it."

Summer sat down in the grass and waited to see if Luke would try to follow her conversation or continue his. He stared at the distant bonfire for a few seconds and then sat next to her without looking at her. "What are you talking about?" he asked.

She put her hand in the grass and pulled out a handful of green. If there was nothing between her and Luke then she didn't have a right to ask what was between him and anyone else. She still wanted to know.

"I'm talking about Lauren."

"What about her?"

"You tell me."

"There's nothing to tell. She worked for us over the summer and then went back to school a few weeks ago. Are you suggesting there was something going on?"

"*She* suggested it by being upset that you were here with me." Summer's voice rose slightly.

"You think she was upset about that?"

Summer rolled her eyes. "She's clearly a little infatuated with you."

"Oh... that's interesting." And a little flattering if true. What Luke found far more interesting though was the fact that Summer seemed to be bothered by it.

"How interesting is it?" She began picking grass faster.

Luke quietly watched her hand attacking the grass. He wasn't sure how to assure her that she had no reason to be jealous without accusing her of being jealous. He thought about putting his hand on top of hers, but was afraid she'd just shake it off. "Summer," he said softly, "I don't understand why you're getting upset."

"I don't understand either," she mumbled. She slipped her hand through her hair to bring it forward to cover part of her face. She

134

thought she was hiding her frustration better. She needed to ask his opinion of their relationship and she was afraid of the answer. Luke didn't have time to say anything else before she continued, a little clearer but still facing away from him. "I thought it was me, that I scared you off by being... clueless. But now we're here and... it doesn't... well, I'm more than a little infatuated and I kind of thought you found that interesting and now I don't know." The pile of plucked grass was growing around her.

He tried to push her hair back and she kept her head bent down so that the hair fell forward as soon as he let go. He pushed it back a few more times, trying to see her face. It wasn't fair at all. She wanted to hide, but his touch was so gentle she couldn't bear to ask him to stop. He seemed to be giving her the answer she wanted and she was still afraid.

"Summer," he said, "I meant it was interesting like the difference between a yam and a sweet potato is interesting. But you are... I don't think I've ever found anything or anyone more interesting. I..." He didn't know if he had been wrong or if she changed her mind, but he could hardly believe what she was saying. She wanted to be with him and she wanted to know that he felt the same way. He pushed her hair back one more time as he whispered, "I think I love you."

Luke only got a glimpse of her smile before it was covered by her beautiful hair. He sat back to see if she'd face him again. After a few seconds, she felt brave enough to stop hiding and look right at him. She was surprised to find those deep blue eyes waiting for her. Her breath caught in her throat as she realized how perfect the moment would be for that kiss she'd been waiting for.

He didn't move or break the connection and yet the space between them seemed to shrink. Summer didn't notice that was because *she* had leaned closer. Luke didn't miss the invitation though. He met her halfway and kissed her before she had time to panic. It was a different emotion that caused her heart to race.

"Wow," she said, barely audible.

Luke smiled self-consciously, "Wow?"

She nodded slightly. She'd tell him eventually, but right then he didn't need to know she didn't have anything for comparison. Summer tried to remember what he had said before she steered the conversation. "What were you going to say before?"

"When?"

"You seemed to be thinking about the fire and you said something about talking him into it?"

"Oh, yeah… that was about my dad. He used to burn leaves every fall and one year I talked him into putting this old, broken clock radio in the fire. It made the thickest, blackest smoke and was so clearly not a good idea. I was only eight or nine and I thought it was funny. I tried to think of other things to throw in the fire, but he'd learned his lesson. He said we were sticking with leaves."

Summer moved just a bit closer so that she could comfortably put her head on Luke's shoulder. It was a ploy to get him to put his hand in the hair tumbling down her back and it worked. She closed her eyes and said, "I've been talking a lot tonight. Tell me another story."

"It's in the truck."

That was not a story. "What's in the truck?"

"I was just remembering that I got you something. I left it in the truck and now I thought… maybe you'd like to have it."

"You got me something? Oh, dear. Now I have a serious dilemma."

He could hear the smile in her voice and doubted the seriousness. "What dilemma?" he asked.

"I really don't want to move because, well, this is nice. On the other hand, I want to know what's in the present."

"Yeah, I see the problem." Luke didn't want to get up either. Watching the fire with his arm around Summer was more than nice. "You said they don't douse the bonfire until midnight, right?"

"That's right."

"It's barely after eight. We could take a walk down the street and come right back."

"Okay," she said.

Luke stood first and offered his hand to help her up. This time he didn't let go.

"Are you going to give me a little hint?"

"I'll tell you one thing. It's what I bought from the crazy woman at the hobby store. I thought she was going to ask you about it."

"Did she help you pick it out?"

"Um, is it bad if I say yes?"

Summer shook her head. As they passed the stage again, they could see a pair of kids around ten or eleven years old trying to do a comedy routine. The walk to Summer's house was still short and she waited

136

patiently while Luke opened his truck and emerged with a small white box in his hand. He kept his eyes on the box as he handed it to her.

The night was going so well now that Summer didn't think there was any way she could be disappointed by the contents. She didn't hesitate to remove the lid. The necklace had three loops at the bottom with bright yellow beads and pale yellow beads the rest of the way around the chain. "It's pretty," Summer said. "And it matches." She handed him the box so she could have both hands to put on the necklace.

He tossed the box onto the seat of his truck. "Can I do it?"

She gave him the necklace and pulled her hair out of the way. He stood close enough to look over her shoulder at the clasp and didn't back up when it was fastened. He gently kissed the side of her neck and then kissed her lips, a little longer than the first time. Summer dropped her hair as she returned the kiss, no practice necessary. Luke smiled at her before he turned to close the door on his truck.

As they started to cross the street, Summer noticed that her family was nearly caught up to them. Kyle was pulling Leo in a wagon and she hoped he had only looked their way at the sound of the door closing. Max was walking behind the wagon with Megan.

"You all calling it a night?" Summer asked as they met on the sidewalk.

"Yes," Max said with an unmistakable pout.

"We had fun," Megan said, "and now it's time for bed. I assume we'll see you a little later, Summer."

"Yeah, we're hoping to find some better entertainment by the time we get back over there."

"Good luck with that," she said. She picked Leo up out of the wagon and ushered Max towards the house.

Kyle had a slight smile and a lot of sarcasm as he said, "I am so glad I was helpful." Then he sighed and began pulling the empty wagon towards the garage. With a wave over his shoulder, he said, "Have fun, but not too much."

When Luke and Summer returned to Yam Fest, they found a band of local teenagers playing some cover songs. The band was not completely terrible so they found a relatively isolated patch of grass that was a little closer to the stage than before. The music was muffled, but their view of the fire was fantastic. Fireflies appeared here and there like sparks escaping. People were laughing in the distance, but Luke and Summer felt alone in the crowd.

"This is more romantic than I pictured," Luke admitted.

"It's ended up that way."

"I should have thought to bring a blanket to sit on though."

"You'll know better next year."

Luke grinned at her. "Are you saying you'll let me take you again next year?"

"I certainly hope you'll ask."

"Me, too." He looked at the fire and said, "It wasn't entirely my fault."

Thank you for reading *Jealousy and Yams*. Reviews are always appreciated.

Also by Amanda Hamm

Andrew's Key (Stories From Harford)

Meet Cute: 5 Romantic Short Stories

The 4th Floor Lounge

Weathering Evan